the new normal

the new normal

ASHLEY LITTLE

ORCA BOOK PUBLISHERS

Library and Archives Canada Cataloguing in Publication

Little, Ashley, 1983-
The new normal / Ashley Little.

Issued also in electronic formats.
ISBN 978-1-4598-0074-8

I. Title.
PS8623.I898N49 2013   jc813'.6   C2012-907449-7

First published in the United States, 2013
Library of Congress Control Number: 2012952945

Summary: Tamar lost her sisters to a drunk driver and her parents to grief. Now she's losing her hair—and possibly her mind.

 MIX
Paper from
responsible sources
FSC **FSC® C004071**
www.fsc.org

 ANCIENT FOREST ™
FRIENDLY

Orca Book Publishers is dedicated to preserving the environment and has printed this book on Forest Stewardship Council® certified paper.

Orca Book Publishers gratefully acknowledges the support for its publishing programs provided by the following agencies: the Government of Canada through the Canada Book Fund and the Canada Council for the Arts, and the Province of British Columbia through the BC Arts Council and the Book Publishing Tax Credit.

Design by Teresa Bubela
Cover photography by Getty Images
Author photo by John Harkin

ORCA BOOK PUBLISHERS
PO Box 5626, Stn. B
Victoria, BC Canada
v8R 6s4

ORCA BOOK PUBLISHERS
PO Box 468
Custer, WA USA
98240-0468

www.orcabook.com
Printed and bound in Canada.

16 15 14 13 • 4 3 2 1

For Mom and Dad

one

I am losing my hair. I don't know why. I'm only sixteen. I'm not starving myself. I'm not undergoing chemotherapy or radiation treatments. But I have been losing shitloads of hair. It started with my pubic hair. I went to the can one morning and a big gob of hair dropped out onto the toilet paper, like a chunk of moss falling off a log. It was horrifying. That was on a Monday. By the end of that week all the fine hairs on my arms and legs had vanished. Now there are bald pink patches on my scalp. I lost my eyelashes. My eyelashes! I went to see my doctor about it. "Wait awhile," he said. "See if it grows back. In the meantime, we'll get inside you for some blood tests." Perv. He said it was probably stress. But I'm not stressed! Well, I wasn't before. *Now* I am about losing my hair. What will be next?

My nails? My teeth? My bone marrow? I see my future self as a shrunken dried-apple-head, with caved-in holes for eyes and a mouth like a cat's asshole. I might as well drop out of high school now and join a frigging circus sideshow.

You can't tell anymore, but I used to have beautiful hair. Mahogany with natural amber highlights. Wavy. When they were younger, my sisters fought over who got to brush it. I brushed it one hundred strokes every night before bed with a genuine boar-bristle hairbrush. Or, if I was feeling charitable, I would let my sisters do it for me. Fifty strokes each, to be fair. Neither of them had hair as nice as mine. They're dead now. Their deaths did not involve hair loss. They died from riding in cars with boys. Stupid, drunken boys. Boys who had to show off, race, play Chicken. Chicken is a moronic game, more dangerous than Russian Roulette. I don't know why my sisters put themselves in that situation, but I'd bet two hundred dollars they did it to look cool. But dead people aren't cool. They're just dead. I'd like to think they couldn't have seen it coming, but when there's a car in your lane flying toward you, that's *all* you see coming. The headlights. The windshield. The darkness. Forever.

I used to say they only got one brain between them because they were twins. Well, live fast, die young, as they say. They were fifteen when they died. I'm still the oldest, but now I'm also the only. The parents are devastated, obviously.

Both of them lost their minds right after the twins died. Mom has completely checked out. All she does is be weird and do yoga and meditation. I guess she's coping the best way she knows how. Sometimes she seems normal again, but if I look closely at her mouth, I can see that her smile is fake. Dad doesn't say much anymore, so I'm not too sure about him. Neither of them has experienced hair loss.

The parents and some of my teachers thought I would have to repeat grade eleven because I missed so much school due to the bereavement period and all. Abby and Alia have been gone eighty-three days now. They died on Halloween. I started going to classes again two weeks ago. At first I thought I'd do correspondence courses, but I wasn't very motivated to do the work, plus everyone thought it best that I do more socializing. I don't make friends easily, because I think most people are useless idiots. I don't see that as being a flaw on my part. There is no such thing as a "people person"; some people are just better at faking niceness. I put in an effort occasionally. I joined the chess club at the start of this year. I'm the only girl in it. All the guys in the club think they're real smart, but only two of them actually are: Brian Walton and Roy Lee. Roy is in grade twelve. He has short black hair with a cowlick in the front and eyes like oil slicks. He's the only member of the chess club I haven't beaten yet. Roy and I are the MVPs in the club.

Every month the chess club participates in tournaments with other high schools in Alberta. Once a year, in January, we send a player to the nationals, where we compete against the best high-school chess players in Canada. It's high pressure, but nothing that would make your hair fall out. Roy got to go to the nationals last week. I wanted to go to cheer him on, but it was in Toronto, and the parents didn't have enough Air Miles, and I couldn't afford the plane ticket. Roy got to fly for free and stay in a fancy-ass hotel. He phoned me from the hotel every night between eight and eight thirty to update me on who was popping power plays, who was coming up stale and what kind of Bobby Fischer-esque drama was going down. Our conversations were usually brief and entirely chess related, but one night he told me about walking on the glass floor at the top of the CN Tower and how he and his dad had dinner there in the revolving restaurant. "It was awesome, Tamar. You can see three-hundred-and sixty degrees out over the whole city. All the lights! I wish you could've seen it."

"Yeah, me too." I cleared my throat. "You know, the Calgary Tower has a restaurant too."

"Oh yeah?"

"It's not as high, but I think it revolves."

"Well...maybe we could check that out when I get back," he said.

"I'd like that." And then there was this sort of long pause that was kind of awkward but kind of nice too, because there was nothing else to say yet neither of us wanted to hang up.

At the end of the week, Roy was ranked fifth-best youth chess player in Canada, and I got a postcard with the CN Tower on it.

Sometimes I think about what it would be like to have a boyfriend, but they're all so frigging immature, I might as well wait a few years. Who wants to be a babysitter, really? Besides, high-school relationships never last more than a month, and the ones that do? Well, usually it turns out one of them is gay. Take Andrea and Scott, for example. They'd been together nearly two years, and they were this picture-perfect couple. She's our school president, and he gets the lead in all the plays. They're both ridiculously good-looking with naturally great hair. Nice, popular, smart. You know, the kind of couple that makes you want to vomit when you see them skipping down the hall holding hands. But last week, it came out (excuse the pun) that Scott is actually gay. Call in the bomb squad, because I'm pretty sure no one saw that coming. Poor Andrea. Her shiny raven hair looks like a matted bird's nest now. I guess it's true what they say: things aren't always what they seem.

Anyway, dating is extremely overrated. It's a sick ploy for guys to show off their fast cars and their fast moves. Where would that leave me? Crunched up in some rank backseat with my pants around my ankles, or splattered all over the pavement like my sisters. Thanks, but I'll pass.

Even if my sisters hadn't been in that particular car on that particular night, they probably would have crashed eventually anyway, because they were always pulling shit like that. People used to call them the evil twins. Because they were both little delinquents and always looking for trouble. I don't even know what all they were into. Heavy stuff. I'm pretty sure they were selling weed. Maybe more. They were very popular. A little too popular, if you know what I mean.

Most people didn't even realize we were related until they died and I was named in their obituaries: *Survived by sister, Tamar.* Doesn't that sound so strange? I had to survive their lives, and now I have to survive their deaths. It's fucked up.

When I went back to school, people who had never spoken to me before, never even given me a second glance, came up to me and said nice things about Abby and Alia. How they were so lovely, such sweethearts, so kind. Which, let's face it, wasn't true. Beautiful, sure. Nice? Not so much. Not to me anyway. And all the kids said they were sorry. Sorry. They all said sorry. As if it was their fault. And I guess, in some ways, maybe it was.

One day I was waiting to use the water fountain, and a girl with a blue mohawk ahead of me spun around, her face crumpled up like a paper bag. She threw her arms around me and started sobbing so hard into the side of my head, I was worried she would knock my bandana off and expose my patchy scalp. And it was all just so dramatic, such a show. I mean, if you're going to be upset over the deaths of my sisters, that's fine, but don't make a production out of it. Don't use it as an excuse to bring attention to yourself.

I think there are two kinds of people: those who want to bring attention to themselves, and those who want to deflect attention from themselves. I happen to fall into the latter category. Which is why this hair-loss thing is a critical pain in the ass for me. Nothing, I guarantee you, *nothing*, could bring a girl more attention than cruising the halls at school with a gleaming chrome dome.

Fortunately, I have been able to hide it thus far through the genius of false eyelashes, bandanas and hats. Mom showed me how to apply false eyelashes, those delicate, spidery things. I perched on the edge of the toilet with a mirror in my lap while Mom did one eye for me; then I tried to attach the other side. My hands were shaky from coffee, and I had to peel the lashes off twice and start over to get them on straight.

"Use the glue sparingly, Tamar, so you can reuse them," Mom said, sharpening an eyebrow pencil.

"How do you know so much about this stuff anyway?" I asked as she traced my eyebrows with clean, firm strokes. Her fingers smelled like strawberries.

"I never told you this?" She turned my face so I could see it in the mirror.

The eyebrows she had drawn looked better than the originals. They had a high and delicate arch and were the color of unpeeled almonds. I wiggled them around.

Scrunched them together. They opened up my face, made my dark eyes stand out.

"Told me what?"

She stepped back to admire her work and smiled a secretive little smile. "I ran for Miss Alberta once."

"*What?*" I almost fell off the toilet. "*When?*"

"It was nineteen seventy-six."

"Did you—?"

"I was a finalist."

Then Mom got this dreamy, faraway look in her eyes and seemed to stand a little taller while she put the makeup away. It made me wonder how many things there are to know about a person, and if you can ever really know them all.

I wished she had won. I wished I could say that my mom was Miss Alberta 1976. That would be something. I looked at her in the bathroom mirror, humming to herself. She was beautiful. I guessed she always had been. She was tall, but soft in all the right places. Her hair, which tapered toward her chin, was the color of new pennies. She had bright green eyes and a sprinkle of freckles across the thin bridge of her nose. Abby and Alia looked like her. I got my dad's looks. All sharp angles and awkwardness, eyes too small and nose too big.

But it doesn't matter. The prettier you are, the more hassles you get. That's why I'm fine being the way I am. The girls aren't jealous and the guys aren't lustful. So it's actually better to be unattractive. Nobody bothers me at all.

"Why don't you come to yoga class with me tonight?" Mom said as she poured us some orange juice.

"Nah."

"I think it could really open you up, Tamar."

I picture someone sawing my torso in half when she says that. Yoga seems to have helped her find some peace, but I don't think stretching can regenerate hair growth.

I have been eating a lot of peanut butter lately. Peanut butter supposedly works miracles for hair growth.

Smooth peanut-butter-and-jelly sandwiches
Crunchy peanut-butter-and-pickle sandwiches
Peanut butter on celery sticks
Peanut butter and cottage cheese on toast
Peanut butter and cheddar cheese on a bun
Apples and peanut butter
Peanut butter on crackers
Peanut-butter cookies
Reese's Peanut Butter Cups
Reese's Pieces
Peanut butter and marshmallows
Peanut butter and honey on toast
Spoonfuls of peanut butter throughout the day

Sometimes I rub peanut butter into my bald spots. I'm still waiting for my miracle.

I have also started praying, really hard. Although I'm not entirely sure if I believe in God, I guess if my hair grows back I will, and if it doesn't, I won't. Ask and ye shall receive, as they say.

Dad renounced God when Abby and Alia were killed. It was strange, because the five of us used to go to church every Sunday and say grace at dinner and all that jazz, but after they were gone it just…stopped. How can you believe in something for all those years, and have all this faith and love and devotion, and then walk away and never look back?

I suspect Dad still talks to God sometimes when he thinks no one is listening. He must talk to somebody, because he sure doesn't talk to us.

He used to be a pretty fun dad. He told us jokes and drew cartoons and made hats and boats and swans out of the newspaper after he had finished reading it. He carved animals out of wood, and when we were little he used to help us make castles and moats out of the furniture. We were the princesses trapped inside the castle, and he was our shining knight come to rescue us on his shoulders. He made us chocolate mud pies and his world-famous spaghetti sauce and colossal cheeseburgers on the barbecue. He took us to the lake and on drives and to movies and out for dinner and ice skating and bowling and hiking and to the zoo. And sometimes he would take us to Banff, just for the day, and we'd get a bag of licorice allsorts from a giant candy store and then drive back home, just because we could. And now, he doesn't do anything. He sleeps for most of the day and then watches TV on the couch or sits out in the garage until three o'clock in the morning, drinking beer and smoking cigarettes.

Mom told me he used to smoke when they first met, but she made him stop because it's disgusting and bad for your health. I guess he doesn't care anymore.

Sometimes I want to take him by the shoulders and shake him and yell in his face, "I'm still here! I'm Tamar, your oldest daughter, and I'm still here!"

I know he loved my sisters more than me, and if I could bring them back for him, I would.

two

Today in biology class we discussed rare diseases, and I thought I'd better get a second opinion about my hair loss. At lunchtime I went to 7-Eleven with Roy to get Coke slushies and dill-pickle chips. Roy was wearing sunglasses. That was irritating, because I couldn't see his eyes. Roy has what my sisters called "story eyes." They used to say you could tell by someone's eyes if they were going to be a significant person in your life. If the eyes reflected you, this was just another stranger passing through your line of sight, but if you saw deeper into their eyes, saw the patterns, the layers, all the flecks and specks and sparkles, you would come to know their story, and maybe even be a part of it. I used to tell my sisters they were so full of shit their eyes were turning brown. But Roy does have supernice eyes: black-brown with flecks of orange layered with green and gold speckles. They're always changing, like a kaleidoscope. I plucked his shades from his face and put them on myself. He pretended not to notice as he flipped through a sleazy men's magazine.

"How come you're always wearing these bandanas now, Tamar? Are you in a gang or something?" Roy asked, sliding the magazine back on the rack.

"No."

"Can I be in your gang?"

"Shut up."

Then he pulled off my bandana, and a big clump of hair came off with it. Roy threw it on the floor as if it were going to attack him. I covered my ugly scalp with my hands. "Fuck you, Roy!"

He scooped up my bandana and stared at it. Neither of us said anything. We just stood there in the 7-Eleven, not talking or moving while the door buzzer bing-bonged loudly as people came and went. We stood there for what felt like three hours but was probably only a minute. Finally, Roy asked in a quiet, broken voice, "Tamar, are you dying?"

I started laughing, but it turned into crying. "I don't know."

We left the 7-Eleven then, without even paying for our slushies, and crossed the crowded parking lot to the field behind our school. We plunked down on the dead, khaki-colored grass. I cried. Roy ripped out grass. I told him everything. About the eyelashes, the peanut butter, the pervy doctor—everything. Because I cried so much, the glue on my false eyelashes melted, and they slid right off. It was utterly humiliating to sit there with no eyelashes, blinking like a newt.

"Have your blood tests come back yet?"

"Yeah, they were all normal."

"That's good, I guess."

"But this"—I pointed to my head—"*this* is not normal!"

"Did you try looking up hair loss online?" Roy asked.

"Of course."

"And?"

"All that came up were ads for Rogaine and phone numbers for cancer support groups. Nobody knows what I have."

"You have to get a second opinion," Roy said. "I'm going to take you to my Uncle Lung. He does acupuncture and works with chi and all that."

I imagined a massive pink lung hurling metal spikes at a giant bull's-eye on my shiny bald head. "No way no how is anyone sticking anything into me."

"You want your hair to grow back, don't you?"

"Yeah."

"Well, don't worry about it then. It'll be okay; you'll see." Then he reached for my hand and held it kind of delicately for a moment, until I pretended to cough and pulled it back.

"We can go right now," he said.

"What about school?"

He shrugged.

"Don't you have a chem test next period?"

"This is more important. Come on." Roy jumped to his feet and grabbed my hand. He yanked me up so fast, the world spun. For a second, I thought I might fall down. I leaned into Roy, and he wrapped his arms around me and squeezed. I buried my head in his chest and hoped I wouldn't get any snot on his hoodie. Then the bell rang, but instead of going back inside the school, we got on the bus and went downtown.

Dr. Lung had a tiny office on 17th Avenue. It wasn't what I had expected, but of course I didn't know what to expect. It smelled like musky herbs and seaweed and rubbing alcohol and burnt hair. There were Chinese paintings of bamboo and poppies and trees, and brass statues of tigers and dragons and Buddha.

Dr. Lung popped up from behind a massive wooden desk, clutching something tightly in his left hand. "Ah, Roy! You have friend." He was a short thin man with thick glasses that made his black eyes look like beetles. He had close-cropped salt-and-pepper hair and square, stained teeth. He wore a white lab coat.

"Yes, Uncle, this is Tamar. She needs your help."

Dr. Lung looked at me for a too-long minute, then pushed his glasses on top of his head. There were deep wrinkles around his eyes, and he squinted at me as he slipped the thing from his hand into his pocket. "Okay, we will help her then," he said. He took a stubby pencil from his desk, wrote something on a sheet of lined yellow paper and gave it to Roy. "Please bring me these things from Chinatown." He handed him a fifty-dollar bill.

"Yes, Uncle." Roy smiled at me and hurried out. Chimes tinkled after him in the doorway.

"Sit down here, Tamar." Dr. Lung rapped the pencil on the chair in front of his desk and sat opposite me. "Now, what is wrong wif you?"

"I—I'm losing my hair." I began to cry.

"Shh, don't worry. You will be okay." He took hold of the undersides of my wrists, one in each hand, and held them firmly. I continued to cry.

"Are you in pain?" he asked.

"No."

"Then why you cry?"

I didn't answer.

"Don't worry. You will be okay. I will help you."

I wanted to believe him.

He let go of my wrists and wrote something on a chart.

"Tongue!" he said, and he dropped his tongue to his chin.

I stuck mine out and he studied it.

"Now, up."

I stood up.

He laughed through his nose. "No, just yo tongue up."

"Oh." I sat back down and jammed the tip of my tongue against the roof of my mouth.

He leaned closer to me, then scribbled again on the chart. "You eat propelly?"

"Yes."

"Yes?"

"I think so."

"Get enough exercise?"

"Does anyone?"

"How is yo energy level?"

"Medium to low, I guess."

"Night sweats?"

"Usually," I said.

"Ringing in yo ears?"

"Sometimes."

"High? Low?"

"High. I thought it was hearing damage from listening to music too loud."

"Nope. Any problems wif menstruation?"

My face burned. My period had become irregular since Abby and Alia died. It had only come once in the past three months, which was okay with me because it meant less hassle. I told him this, and he wrote it down.

"Loose stool?" he asked.

"What?"

"Stool. Shit. Crap. Scat. Excrement."

"Um, sometimes."

"How do you feel?"

"Scared," I said.

"Come wif me."

He led me into a small white room. A white massage table stood in the middle of the room. There was a hole at one end for your face. A miniature rock fountain was plugged into the wall, and a stereo played fluty music. I smelled something sickly sweet and vaguely familiar. Incense. The same scent Mom burns when she does her yoga, which lately is all day, every day. Dr. Lung handed me a white sheet and told me to take my clothes off and lie face down, with the sheet over me, and he would come back in a few minutes. It was cold in the room, and a shiver ran through me as I stripped to my bra and panties.

When he returned, he told me to take deep breaths. "Since this is yo first treatment, I will only use a few needles, maybe fifteen, sixteen."

That seemed like a hell of a lot of needles to me.

"Now relax," he said, and he ran his hand over my back. His skin felt like paper. I stared down through the head-hole at the cracked, gray-yellow tiles that had once been white. I held my breath. I felt the cool dampness of an alcohol-soaked cotton ball, then a sharp pinch at the base of my spine. Then one in each shoulder blade. Two in the backs of my knees. I peeked around and saw that he was using a small golden hammer to punch the needles through my skin.

He swiped with the cotton ball and then tapped a needle into the space below my ankle bone. Then one in the other foot. One in the center of my lower back that caused a stabbing burst of pain. "Ow!" I yipped. It took all my willpower not to reach around and yank that needle out. Instead, I whimpered into the head-hole.

"Breeve," Dr. Lung said. "Always remember to breeve."

He said that that was enough for now and that he would leave the needles in me for a few minutes, come back, take them out and do my front. He told me to lie still and relax. Then I heard the door click shut. My entire back felt prickly and hot. I felt sick. The needle in my lower back still hurt. I could feel it pulsating. The *pish-pish* sound from the rock fountain was making me need to pee so badly, I could feel my molars floating. The flute music had become high pitched—like a piccolo—and it was irritating the hell out of me. I stretched out my arm to turn the stereo off, but I couldn't reach it. I tried again, straining my fingers toward the Power button. If I'd had long fingernails, I could have done it. But they were bitten to the quick, and the screechy music played on. I let my arm fall. Suddenly I felt exhausted, like I would never be able to do anything again. As if the weight of the sky was bearing down on me. It seemed like Dr. Lung had been gone for hours. I was thirsty, and my mouth was dry and tasted like sawdust. When Dr. Lung finally came back, he exclaimed, "Ah! Very good! The chi is moving."

I touched my arm to feel if hair was growing back. It wasn't. "What do you mean?" I asked.

"Your chi. I can see it moving." He didn't explain further and began taking needles out with quick flicks of his wrist. He wiped the point on my lower back with another cotton ball. It must have bled.

"Now on yo back, please." He selected long thin needles from a clear plastic case. I flipped onto my back, and he gave me another small white sheet to cover my chest and moved the large sheet down to my hips. My skin was goose flesh. Using the small golden hammer, he placed a needle into the center of each of my wrists; into the skin between the thumb and first finger of each of my hands; into my stomach, quite deep, below my belly button; into each of my shins; and between my eyebrows—or where my eyebrows used to be. He told me to relax, then closed the door quietly behind him.

The CD finally whirred to a stop, and an eerie stillness filled the room. I stared at the three-inch steel needles quivering in my wrists. The needle in my belly rose and fell with each breath I took. I felt like I was floating in the center of that white room, and the walls floated around me. I felt a warm tingling between my legs. I thought about Roy. I wondered if he knew he was my best friend. I wondered how it would feel to kiss him on the lips. I thought about my sisters, wondering if they could see me right now, and how, if they could see me, they would be laughing at me.

Dr. Lung returned and removed the needles. They made sharp sucking sounds as they came out of me. The sounds made me feel sicker. I was hot and thirsty, and the room seemed to be shrinking around me. I wanted to lie there until I felt normal again, but Dr. Lung told me to get dressed and meet him in the front room.

When I came out, Dr. Lung was smoking a cigarette. I sat in the chair in front of his desk again. He handed me a hot white cup. "Drink," he said. I had no idea what was in the cup, but I drank it anyway. It was bitter.

"No swimming, no bathing for the rest of today, okay?"

"Okay."

"Good. Now, you take these herbs. Every day, okay?" He passed me a red bottle with Chinese characters on it.

"Okay." I wanted to know what the pills were, but I didn't ask.

"Now, you don't pay today because yo Roy's friend. If you come back next week, it will be fifty."

"Fifty bucks?!"

He laughed. "Fifty bucks. Yes. Bucks."

"Should I come back?"

"That's up to you," he said. "See how you feel after today."

I nodded. Tears blinded me and spilled onto the desk.

"Tamar, you will be okaaay! Don't worry!" He took my hands in his and squeezed them.

"Thank you."

"Yo welcome."

The chimes above the door jingled, and Roy came in, smelling like cold, fresh air. He placed a brown paper bag on the desk and handed Dr. Lung some change.

"I think I got it all," Roy said. "Ready to go?" he asked, turning to me.

"Yeah."

Roy thanked his uncle and I thanked him again and we went out into the street. The sky was drained of color; it was windy, and the air was crisp. It felt like it might snow.

three

A scabby old man with a shopping cart full of bottles and cans pushed up against me as he passed us.

"Got a dollar for me, sweetie?" His putrid breath hung in the air.

I clutched my purse and shook my head no.

"How 'bout yer fella?" He turned to Roy. The man's jaw hung slack, showing his brown, rotted teeth.

Roy dug a dollar out of his pocket and held it out.

"Much obliged, sir." The man bowed and lifted his cap, showing a scaly, bald head. Then he clattered on down the sidewalk, whistling "Ring-Around-the-Rosie." I felt as if somebody was walking over my grave. If I'd had any hair left on the back of my neck, it would've stood up.

My sisters and I used to hold hands and dance around in a circle, singing that song:

Ring around the rosie
A pocket full of posies
Ashes, ashes
We all fall down!

Then we'd pull each other down to the ground as hard as we could. I rubbed my eyes, trying to wipe the image out of my head. I could still hear the man with the cart, whistling down the sidewalk.

"Want to go for a bubble tea?" Roy asked, turning to me.

"A what?"

He laughed.

I had never had it before. Roy insisted that I try it, so we walked to a little bubble-tea café. Roy ordered, and I sat down at a small round table, rubbed my palms together and stared out the window at two thin brunettes sharing a cigarette.

"Earth to Tamar!" Roy said, placing a cup with a straw in it on the table in front of me. "Do you read?"

I rolled my eyes and drew a sip of tea through the straw. It was squidgy and lukewarm and actually pretty nasty, but I told Roy I liked it because I didn't want to hurt his feelings, and you should never look a gift horse in the mouth.

"So, do you feel any different?" Roy asked.

"I always feel different."

"You know what I mean."

"I guess I feel…a sort of relief."

"Yeah?"

"You know, like when your bike tires are too full and then you let a little bit of air out and it's a better ride?"

"Uh-huh…"

"I don't know. I don't know if it even does anything. I mean, how could it? Really."

"Well, that's the great thing about acupuncture. Uncle Lung says you don't have to believe in it for it to work."

Some grade-twelve girls from our school came in then, and Roy craned his neck to watch them as they flounced up to the counter and ordered their disgusting teas. They were chatty and giddy and talking too loud. They tossed their perfect hair over their perfect shoulders or tucked it behind their perfect ears. I hated them all.

"Let's go." I got up and dropped my still-full cup into the garbage can and stood by the door, buttoning my coat. Roy's gaze lingered on the girls as we left.

The sky had darkened to a leaden gray. We said nothing. Our breath formed silver clouds in the air between us. We walked to the C-train and stood on the platform with our hands jammed in our pockets. The platform was full of businesspeople in suits, carrying briefcases, looking pinched and worried, checking their watches every three seconds. I don't know what I want to be when I grow up, but I know I don't want to be one of them.

We got on the next southbound train. There were some idiot punk kids on the train, swinging from the poles and hollering obscene jokes at each other. Blue-mohawk girl from school was there. She nearly kicked me in the face when she did a backflip over the top handrail. I wished the C-train cops would come and bust her stupid ass. Roy and I didn't bother talking over the din of the punks.

When we got off at Anderson station, Roy's bus was just pulling away from the curb. We both ran to stop it, waving our arms wildly. The driver shook his head but opened the door for Roy to get on.

"Roy," I yelled. "Thank you!" The door banged closed.

Roy pressed his palm against the glass window as the bus lurched away.

I waited alone in the cold for the bus to Canyon Meadows as the sky turned from gray to black.

When I stepped off the bus, it was dark.

"There you are," said a male voice from the bench at the bus stop.

I peered through the darkness at the guy. I didn't know him. I pressed my lips together tight and speed-walked away.

"Hey! I'm talking to you." Suddenly he was at my side, tall and beefy with a pug face and a shaved head. He wore a black leather jacket, with spikes on the shoulders, and Doc Martens.

"I'm sorry. I think you have me mixed up with someone else."

"You're Tamar Robinson aren't you?"

I kept walking fast. Looking straight ahead. My heart exploding in my throat. "Who wants to know?"

He chuckled. "Let's just say I'm a friend of your sisters."

"They're not…"

"I know, I know. Condolences and all that. But debts don't die when people do, girlie. Sorry to say."

"Look, I don't know anything about—"

"Listen." He grabbed my arm, hard. "They owed me a thousand dollars, all right?"

I stopped walking and tried to pull my arm back, but he had a vise-like grip on me.

"Maybe I could've let it slide if it had been less than that, but I have to pay people too, you know? And this is putting a BIG hole in my profit margins. Sorry, girlie, but the weight falls on you. Unless you think I should ask your parents for it…"

"No."

"I need it a week from today. In cash. Got it?"

I ripped my arm away and took off down the street.

"I know where you live!" he yelled after me.

I hoofed it home as fast as my legs would carry me. When I slammed through the door, the parents were sitting at the kitchen table. Dad had his head on the table, resting on his forearms, and Mom had this look on her face like she'd been punched in the stomach. They couldn't help me. They couldn't even help themselves. I didn't say hi or take off my coat or anything. I went straight up to my room, closed the door and shoved my dresser in front of it, just in case Pug Face broke in. My hands were shaking. My heart was thudding so hard I could feel it inside my skull. *A thousand dollars. In cash.*

I flopped down on my bed and closed my eyes. I was tired. I was tired of school and tired of home and tired of having two dead sisters. I wished there were some way I could hit *Rewind* and go back to a time when the three of us were best-best-best friends and they worshipped me and I adored them and we played Barbies and Lego and Crazy Eights all day.

But there was no going back. This was my reality: I was sixteen and being hunted by a drug dealer. My hair was falling out and my sisters were dead and my parents were broken and there wasn't a goddamn thing I could do about any of it.

four

On Monday I was late for school. It's true what they say about Mondays—they suck. They always have, and they always will. My first class was Drama, and the teacher, Ms. Jane, asked me to stay after class. Ms. Jane had curly hair the color of taffy, and it was always a frizzy mess. I figured she was going to give me grief about being late, but she didn't.

"Tryouts for the spring play are coming up this week, Tamar."

"Yeah." So what? I thought.

"I think it would be excellent if you auditioned. You've shown real potential in your monologue projects this year."

"What's the play?"

"*The Wizard of Oz.*"

I smiled, because my favorite movie is *Return to Oz*, which is sort of a perverse sequel to the original.

"This is the audition piece for female cast members." She handed me a sheet of paper. It was Dorothy's ramble at the very end, about how it wasn't a dream, it was a real live place. *And you and you and you...and you were there.*

"I don't know, Ms. Jane. I can't really carry a tune."

"That's all right, actually, because we're doing the nonmusical version."

"Oh."

"Just promise me you'll consider it."

"Okay."

"Fabulous! Auditions will be held here in the theater at four o'clock this Friday."

"Okay."

"Hope to see you there!"

I folded the piece of paper and put it inside *1984*, the book we were reading for English. Then I pushed through the theater doors and out into the crowded hallway, where hundreds of students scurried around like rats in a maze.

I found five bucks someone had dropped in the cafeteria and shoved it in my pocket. Only $995 to go. By Friday. If only I could find a way to get every kid in school to give me a dollar, I'd have a grand by the end of today. Maybe I could set up some kind of booth. Have a bucket and a bell like the Salvation Army Santas. For the price of a bag of chips you can save a bald girl from her dead sisters' drug dealer!

After school, I went to the bank and cleaned out my savings account. Ninety-two dollars and seventy-six cents. It was everything I'd saved from birthday and Christmas money, odd jobs and allowance. And now I had to give it all to some dipshit dealer. It was amazing to me that Abby and Alia could still manage to piss me off and screw me over from their graves.

On Tuesday I went to chess club and played against Roy, even though I knew I would lose. I told him I might audition for *The Wizard of Oz*.

"That's cool, Tamar. I think you'd be great."

"Really?"

"For sure. Well, better than you are at chess anyway." He laughed.

"You're a jerk," I said. But I didn't mean it.

After Roy won, I started a game with Brian Walton. Brian's a nervous little grade-eleven guy with greasy glasses, shaggy hair the color of straw and tragic acne, but no one denies that he's probably a genius. My mom met Brian once at a school fundraiser thing. She said he was cute in a super-geek kind of way, and to be extra nice to him because he might end up being my boss someday.

"How are you, Tamar?"

"Not too bad, Brian. How's it going?"

"Good, and you?"

"Um, you already asked me that."

"Oh. Sorry." He moved his knight out, and we didn't speak again until the end of the game when we both said "Good game" at the same time and shook hands. His hand was slimy and gross, and I didn't want to shake it, but those were the rules of the chess club. Every game had to end with a shake. Brian beat me too, but not as badly as Roy had. They say that every game makes you a better player, no matter if you win or lose, so I guess it wasn't a total waste of a lunch hour. I decided to go outside and get some fresh air before my next class. I walked out the back doors, where all the kids with their puffy jackets and sideways hats and dark bandanas huddled around, smoking and spitting and talking trash. I walked onto the field, turned around and realized they were all staring at me. It's probably my bandana, I thought. They're probably thinking I'm down with a rival gang or something. Shit. Maybe it's time to get a wig. My heart hurt when I thought that, because it was like admitting defeat.

There were still some long, stringy pieces of hair clinging to the back of my skull, creating the illusion that I had hair, but up top I was as bare as a baby's ass. I was losing more and more hair every day, and soon I would be completely, utterly, undeniably bald. I sighed and looked up at the cloudless sky. An airplane's white streak sliced through it like an ugly scar.

The bell rang and I cut through the huddled mass of kids.

"Hey! Who you claimin', girl?" a guy in a black bandana yelled.

"*Please*, that bitch ain't shit," said a fat chick dressed in white.

"She's got a hefty debt though!"

"No doubt!"

Then there was harsh laughter from all around, like gravel in a washing machine. I ducked inside, refusing to look at anyone.

So they knew. Everyone knew. I wondered what would happen if I couldn't get the money by Friday. Would Pug Face and his crew beat me to mush with baseball bats? Cut my face open? Burn my house down?

I walked home after school, scouring the sidewalk for change. I found a nickel and three pennies. Pug Face would just have to accept installments. There was no way I could get the money by Friday. No freakin' way.

On Wednesday night, I talked to my mom about getting a wig.

"Have you considered just shaving the rest of your hair off and wearing it like that lovely Irish woman?"

"What?"

"You know…" She started singing, "*Nothing compares! NoTHING COMPARES…*"

"Stop!" I covered my ears.

"*To you!*"

"No."

"Alia did that, remember? In grade seven, she shaved her head and dyed her scalp purple? She looked great!"

"I can't pull that off, Mom! I *need* hair!"

"Sinéad! That's her name. Sinéad O'Connor."

"No Sinéad, Mom."

"All right," she sighed. "I just want you to understand that wigs made from human hair are very expensive, so we might not be able to get you the one you want. Money's a bit tight right now." She chewed her lower lip.

"This is important!" I slammed my mug of tea down on the counter, and some tea splashed onto my shirt.

"I know it is, honey, I know. Come here." She reached toward me, but I turned away from her and ran upstairs to my room.

Since the accident, my parents had both been off work. My dad was the manager of a Honda dealership, and Mom was a dental hygienist. I didn't know what kind of benefits they were paid or if they'd run out. We had been eating a lot of casseroles lately, so I figured they probably had. Well, shit, they had credit cards, didn't they? I could pay them back. With interest. I would get an after-school job. I would pawn my CDs. I would collect bottles if I had to. I was getting a wig. End of story.

When I got home from school on Thursday, I memorized the audition monologue and practiced it in front of the mirror a few times. I wondered if I should do it lying down, since Dorothy is in bed at the end of the play. I practiced it once lying in bed, but I decided against auditioning that way, because your voice changes when you lie down, and you can't project as well. I wondered if I'd get a part. If I did, I hoped it wouldn't be as a Munchkin. Afterward I took the Yellow Pages and the cordless up to my room and made a few calls to get quotes on human-hair wigs. The cheapest one I found was $590, on sale from $700. The store was in Kensington, and I planned to drag Mom there on the weekend and force her to buy me a wig.

After dinner I got my bike out of the garage and rode down to Fish Creek. The wind shrieked in my eardrums. Black blotches of clouds drooped over the park. I landed a few jumps and flew down a single track, then stopped on the bridge to watch the icy water rush over the rocks. I thought about my sisters. What would they do in my situation?

I rode home, put my bike away and locked it up. I couldn't do it. I couldn't sell my mountain bike to pay their debt. She was my horse, my prized possession, my Black Beauty. And she was mine. There had to be another way.

I had little moths flitting around in my stomach all day Friday. It was a rough day, because I had a math test, a biology quiz and a history test, and I hadn't studied for any of them because I had been too busy practicing the monologue and trying to come up with a grand.

The day dragged on, and I kept expecting Pug Face to pop up from behind a desk with a machete or something.

Finally, the school day was over. I had some time to kill before the four o'clock audition, so I went to Dairy Queen and got a hot-fudge sundae. I sat by the window and watched all the kids coming out of school and breaking off into little groups of two or three or four. I saw the kids who had hassled me on Tuesday and gave them the finger. Even though they couldn't see it, it felt good. F-them and F-Pug Face. He would just have to deal with it.

I ate one last big spoonful of sundae and pressed my tongue to the roof of my mouth to stop the brain freeze that followed. I thought about my visit to Dr. Lung. I had been taking the herbs he'd given me and noticed that I had a little more energy than usual. But maybe it was just nervous energy—after all, I had a massive debt to pay, an audition to get through and a new wig to acquire. I went back to the theater. There were kids sitting on benches or walking around talking to themselves—rehearsing, I guess. Everyone looked nervous as hell. One of the weirdo goth chicks in grade twelve was the stage manager, and she gave me a piece of paper with a number on it and wrote my name on her clipboard. I was number seven. She smiled at me with her freaky black lips and flipped her dried-out black hair over one shoulder.

I walked down the hall to the water fountain and took a long cool drink.

"Save some water for the whales, eh!" said a guy behind me. I could feel my face flush as I stood up and wiped my chin with my sleeve. I knew it was one of Pug's henchmen by the way he was dressed. Baggy black pants, black hoodie and black bandana. Same uniform as Pug Face. He scowled when he saw it was me.

"Hey. Mac says to tell you, be at your bus stop tonight at seven. Bring the cash. Come alone."

I felt a bitter surge in my belly and ran down the hall to the bathroom. I nearly smacked into a massive rugby player named Eric Gaines. He'd been a friend of my sisters and was always really friendly to me. "Whoa! Where's the fire, Tamar?" he called as I zoomed past.

I made it to the toilet just in time to vomit my ice cream sundae into it. I rinsed my mouth and washed my face. *Don't cry. Don't cry. Don't cry.* I took deep breaths and stared at myself in the mirror. "You're going to be okay," I told my reflection. I bit down hard on my lip to keep the tears away.

I got back to the theater just in time to hear goth girl call my number. I looked at the black abyss that was the door to backstage and felt the sickness well up inside me again. I swallowed it back and stood up, straightening my shirt and adjusting my bandana. My hands were shaking as I walked onto the stage. I desperately needed to pee.

There were three people sitting together in the center of the theater, but I couldn't see their faces because a spotlight was shining directly into my eyes. No matter where I stood or where I looked, that spotlight was blinding me. It was so bright, brighter than the sun.

"Name, please?" It sounded like Ms. Jane, but I couldn't be sure because I couldn't see a damn thing.

"Tamar Robinson."

"Thank you. When you're ready, Tamar."

I coughed and cleared my throat so it wouldn't catch during my monologue, and I pushed the flittering moths down into the basement of my body. I gave myself a little shake and then jumped right into it.

"Oh, Auntie Em! Auntie Em!"

And a funny thing happened while I was doing the monologue. I wasn't even thinking of the words at all. I wasn't thinking of how nervous I was or what came next or what facial expressions to wear. I wasn't thinking about the past or my sisters or Pug Face or my hair loss or any of it. It was like I became someone else for a few minutes—I became Dorothy, and I was just there in that bedroom in Kansas, telling them all how it went down in Oz. I was totally, 100 percent, there. And I liked that.

When I was finished, the voice said, "Thank you, Tamar. Cast list will be posted in the hall a week from Monday."

And that was it. No "Good job," no "What part would you like to play?" Just "See ya later—don't let the door hit you on your way out." I thought for sure I hadn't made the cut.

As I was walking home, it started to rain. Then it started to hail. Some of the hailstones were as big as golf balls, and I could hear metal denting as they dropped on cars. I pulled my jacket up over my head and ran at top speed all the way to my house. When I burst through the door, Dad was standing in the living room, staring out the window. He was wearing his ratty green robe and drinking a glass of whiskey.

"Hi," I said.

He looked at me and gave me a meager little half smile.

"Where's Mom?" I asked. "Yoga?"

"Right."

He turned back to the window and I stood beside him, and we looked out on to the street. The hail pummeled the roof and bounced off the sidewalk. A black cat ran across the street and hailstones pounded its head. I felt a little bit sorry for it, even though I hate cats. I'm deathly allergic to them, and they make my lungs seize up. Dad says they're my kryptonite. My sisters used to give me a really hard time about being allergic to cats because they desperately wanted one.

"Why can't you just get a shot?"

"Why don't you just hold your breath?"

"Why don't you just go live in the shed and the cat can live in the house with us?"

"Shut up."

"No, you shut up."

"You shut up first."

And it would go on like that. From the time they were about twelve, they started ganging up on me, and things were never the same after that. There was never anyone to take my side, and the two of them almost always got their way.

We did end up getting a cat, a hairless cat. The breeder claimed it was hypoallergenic. It was the most hideous thing in the world, and I was still allergic to it. Alia named it Skinny. We kept it about a week to see if I could adapt, but finally I went on strike. I set up a tent in the backyard and refused to come inside until the parents agreed to get rid of the cat, which apparently was a difficult decision for them.

"Are you coming in for dinner, Tamar?" my mom had called out to me.

"Are you getting rid of the cat?"

"Well, we have to discuss that, honey."

"What's to discuss? I can't breathe!"

My sisters had already fallen in love with the ugly sack of skin, and they bawled like banshees when he had to leave. You would think I had chopped off their arms by the way my whole family treated me after that. I don't think the twins ever forgave me for ousting Skinny, and they never let me forget it either.

I turned back to my dad. He was unshaven and his eyes looked tired; they were gray with shards of blue, like the sky.

"Dad, I need some money."

He rummaged around in the pockets of his jogging pants, pulled out a crumpled five-dollar bill and held it out to me.

I looked down at it, but I didn't take it.

"I need nine hundred and two dollars."

He put the five back in his pocket and shrugged. "I don't have that."

I sighed.

"May I ask what you need nine hundred and two dollars for?"

"A wig." Obviously, I couldn't tell him it was for my sisters' drug debt.

"What? Why? Did you get invited to a ball at the royal palace?"

"No."

"You going to a fancy costume party? Or hosting a telethon or something?"

"No."

"Then what the heck do you need a nine-hundred-and-two-dollar wig for?"

I pulled off my bandana and looked down at the carpet.

"*Jesus*," he said under his breath.

I realized then that he hadn't even known! I had taken it for granted that Mom had told him, but she obviously hadn't. He had no idea. He put his arms around me and pulled me into him. The ice cubes in his glass clinked behind my back, and a couple of tears slid down my face. Even though he stank of whiskey and B.O., I wanted to stay there for a very long time. I started sobbing then. I couldn't help it.

"It's gonna be okay, Tamar. You'll be all right. Don't cry."

But he didn't know that—no one did—and I cried into his chest as hailstones ricocheted off the windows of our house.

five

It was six eighteen on Friday night, and I had forty-two minutes to come up with $902 or face certain torture and possibly death by Pug Face and his crew. I thought about forging a check, but I couldn't find Mom's checkbook anywhere. She must have taken it to yoga. Plus he'd said cash. Cash. Cash. Cash. The poster on Alia's wall of Johnny Cash giving someone the finger popped into my head, and I found myself in her room for the first time since the funeral.

I flicked on the light and there lay my salvation, shining on her unmade bed. Alia's electric guitar: a metallic-blue Fender. Worth at least fifteen hundy. Pug Face would have to accept it. It was all I had to offer. Hell, I would even throw in the amp for good measure.

I put on three sweaters under my winter coat to pad myself against the hail. I grabbed my bike helmet as an afterthought; the last thing I needed was head trauma as a result of hailstone impact. The theme song to *Jeopardy!* filled the house as I snuck out the back door with Alia's guitar zipped safely inside its case.

I lugged the guitar and amp to the bus stop, stopping partway there to put on my helmet. I pulled my hood up over it so I didn't look like a total freak show, just someone with a very large head. The street was littered with fat white hailstones, and car alarms shrieked all over the neighborhood.

I could see the orange glow of a cigarette as I approached the bus-stop bench. I could tell it was Pug Face by the spikes on his jacket. He was alone. And as far as I could see, he was not carrying a baseball bat. I breathed a sigh of relief. Maybe he would spare me after all.

"She shows," he said.

"Here." I thrust the guitar into his hands and set the amp on the bench.

His eyebrows lifted into his hood. He unzipped the case and ripped out Alia's pride and joy, examining it under the amber glow of the streetlight. "Wow. A left-handed Fender Strat. What the fuck am I supposed to do with this?"

"I don't know. Sell it. Play it. Whatever. It's yours."

"What about the cash?" He fiddled with the guitar strings.

"This is all I have that's worth anything, okay? And it's probably worth more than a thousand. You can have the amp too." I patted the amp for emphasis.

"You know this wasn't the deal, girlie." He stepped toward me, and I opened my mouth to scream for help. But then this hot bubble welled up from somewhere deep inside me.

"Look, man, my sisters made the deal with you, and they're dead. My parents are broke, and I have a rare, incurable disease. There's no money for you. This is it. Take it or leave it."

He looked down at his boots, then back up at me, a smirk smeared across his ugly face.

"What?" I said.

"You remind me of them. Little hard-asses, they were."

"It was Alia's guitar," I mumbled.

"Well, I'll think of her when I'm playing it then," he said as he slung the case across his back. "Chin up, girlie. Life's for the living." He punched me softly in the shoulder, picked up the amp and walked away, his boots crunching over the hailstones.

That night I dreamed that Pug Face kissed me. We were making out, but then he started eating my face. He swallowed my head and chewed it up and spat it out. Scraps of my head lay scattered on the grass; my eyeballs rolled down the sidewalk. Then I dreamed that my hair started to grow back, but it went crazy and kept growing and growing and growing like mad until it filled up the whole house. Abby and Alia were still alive and in their beds, and my hair grew into their rooms and encircled their throats and choked them to death in their sleep. The same thing happened to the parents, but they suffocated because there was no more oxygen to breathe, only hair. They drowned in hair.

I woke up gasping for breath and sat up in bed. I rubbed my head to make sure it had been a dream. A few wisps caught in my fingers and came out in my hands. I turned on my bedside lamp and looked down at my pillow. There were two sad-looking clumps of hair on it. I looked into my mirror and then wished I hadn't. I saw a pathetic alien creature. My hair was all gone now. All of it. I was completely bald. I stared into the mirror, horrified. My ears stuck out like an elf's, and my nose was huge and bulbous. Even my teeth looked bigger. I shut off the light and closed my eyes in the darkness of my total and utter despair.

In the morning, I went downstairs and found Mom sitting cross-legged on the floor of the living room with her eyes closed. She seemed to be humming very, very quietly.

"Mom," I whispered.

No response.

"MOM!"

That gave her a little jolt. She opened her eyes slowly, as if they had been glued shut, and looked up at me with zero recognition, which was scary.

"Earth to Mom. Hello?"

"Hello," she said quietly.

"Emergency wig shopping needs to happen today. This morning."

"Tamar, we talked about this. You know the financial situation."

"Doesn't matter. Doesn't matter. You can put it on your credit card. I'll get an after-school job and pay you back, no problem. This needs to happen *today*, Mom. I'm not screwing around anymore. Are you taking me, or am I going alone?"

She stood up and plucked the black woolen cap off my head. She examined my head closely and then pressed her palm flat against my scalp and rubbed it. She blinked her eyes hard, like she was blinking away tears. "I'm taking you. Get your coat."

"Have you had breakfast?" she asked when we were in the car.

"No, I never eat breakfast."

"You need to eat breakfast, Tamar. Breakfast is the most important meal of the day."

"I haven't eaten breakfast in ten years," I said.

"And look where it's gotten you!"

I laughed and so did she, because it was wholly ridiculous. The entire situation was totally tragic and absurd. She pulled into the drive-through at the Hortons, and I ordered a peanut-butter donut and a coffee, even though I'm not supposed to drink coffee because it stunts your growth. That's the least of my problems right now. I've got bigger fish to fricassee.

When we got to the wig shop, which was called Uptown Hair 'n Accessories, there was a sign taped to the door that said *Back in ten minutes*.

"Shit!"

"It's okay, honey, we'll just wait." She started doing some side stretches right there in front of the store.

"Mom!"

"We must practice our patience, Tamar."

I was running out of patience. With my mom. With my disappearing hair. With everything. We waited around, and then we waited some more. I started pacing. The longer we stood out there in the wind, the more upset I became. My heart beat faster as I paced in front of the store. I was hot and sweaty, so I took off my jacket. I couldn't breathe through my nose anymore—I had to just suck in air through my mouth and then blow it all out like I was blowing up a balloon. I got dizzy and sat down on the curb so I wouldn't fall down. I felt desperate and lonely and ugly and anxious and miserable and pathetic and scared.

Mom came and sat down next to me.

"How am I gonna do this, Mom? How am I gonna get through this?" I clung to her like a small frightened animal.

She took my face in her hands and held my eyes with her own. "Courage, my love. Courage."

Finally, a woman with poufy yellow hair and a little rat dog came and unlocked the door. The dog was wearing a pink-and-black-checkered coat that matched the woman's scarf. She unlocked the door for us and made some irritatingly cheerful comments about the weather. She had so much makeup on that you couldn't see her skin.

"Let me know if I can help you with anything!" she chirped.

"Actually, my daughter needs a wig."

"Any color you like," she said, waving her frosted pink fingernails in the direction of the back wall, full of rainbow, fluorescent and sparkly costume wigs.

"Do you have any human hair?" I asked.

"Short or long?"

"Medium."

"What color?"

"Mahogany. With natural amber highlights."

"Okay...very specific." She looked at my mom with amusement, and I wanted to slap the rouge right off her face. She had *no* idea.

"You could try a different color, Tamar. You know, switch it up a little." Mom peeled a blond bob off a plastic head and held it out to me. "Do you like this one?"

"No."

"Come on, try it on." She shook the wig at me like she was a cheerleader and it was a pom-pom. "Just for fun."

Fun? *Fun?* Because losing every single hair on my body and having to buy a wig and pretend like I hadn't was *fun?* Right.

She thrust the wig into my hands, and the saleswoman pointed me toward a full-length mirror. When I slid off my toque, I heard the woman suck in a sharp breath. I put the blond mop on and looked in the mirror.

"Whoa." I looked like a scrawny Marilyn Monroe impersonator. I tried a pout. Then I got a weird feeling inside, like I was one of those ultra-vain Barbie wannabe-princess types. I didn't like it. I looked at the rat dog. It growled at me and started to vibrate. I turned back to the mirror and shook my head around a little. Maybe it's true what they say, I thought. Maybe blonds *do* have more fun. In any case, I wasn't going to find out. The blond didn't match my skin tone or my eyes. Plus, it was just so…blond.

"Do you have anything darker?" I put the bob back on the creepy plastic head.

"I think you might like one of these." The woman had lined up three brunette heads. "This one is dark chocolate with caramel highlights." She fit it onto my head and adjusted it around my ears.

"Sounds good enough to eat!" Mom said, laughing a little too loudly.

The three of us looked at my reflection. It was pretty hair, but it still looked fake, too overdone. I slid it off and handed it to the woman.

"This one is called burnt sienna. It's a really lovely piece—lots of red undertones." She winked at my mom. I hated the wig woman and her matching dog.

The red one was stick straight and nearly reached my bum, way longer than my real hair would be. Too obvious.

"I like that one on you, honey."

"Yeah, it would be okay if this was nineteen seventy-four!" I curled a piece of the hair around my pinkie. It felt thin and dry. It was too long and too straight. I took it off and scratched my head. I was getting itchy and hot.

"Now this one is called double espresso. We just got it in. I think it will look stunning on you." The woman put it on me and adjusted a few strands around my face, then stood back and looked at me and clapped her hands together. "Ah! I was right!" She beamed.

I stepped around her to look in the mirror. The wig was dark, dark brown, almost black. It shone when the light hit it. It fell to my shoulders and was neither too straight nor too curly, nor too thick or too thin. I touched the individual strands. They felt soft but strong. I gathered them into a ponytail, looking at it from the sides. I let it down. It was good. It made my eyes look shiny and bright. I turned to Mom. She nodded once and a quick smile lit up her face.

"How much is it?" I asked the lady.

"This one is seven sixty-nine plus tax."

"Ohhh." I looked at the rat dog sprawled in the middle of the floor with its tongue hanging out. It let out a little groan too and wiped at its eyes with its paws.

"We'll take it," Mom said, slapping her credit card down on the counter.

I grinned and turned back to the mirror.

The woman sat me down and thinned the wig out a bit with a razor tool so it would look more natural and shapely. Then she gave me wig-care instructions and threw in a roll of special double-sided adhesive tape to keep the wig from falling off. While she was talking, I realized that *she* was wearing a wig, and it made me feel a tiny bit smug. Because I knew that my wig looked better on me than hers did on her.

"Want to wear it out, or should I box it up?"

"I'll wear it."

As Mom reversed out of the parking stall, she said, "Tamar, your dad and I will contribute five hundred dollars toward your new…accessory. But you'll have to make up the difference on your own."

"That's no problem."

"Great."

"Mom?"

"Hmm?"

"Thank you."

She looked at me, her pretty green eyes glistening with tears, and I hoped she wouldn't cry, because then I wouldn't be able to stop myself. I was getting sick and tired of crying.

When we got home, Mom went upstairs to change for yoga and I went to the bathroom to fiddle with my wig in the mirror.

"Where's your dad?" Mom hollered.

I shrugged into the mirror and tossed my head around a bit.

"What?"

"I DON'T KNOW!" I yelled.

I heard her thump down the stairs and go to the kitchen. Probably checking the fridge for a note. Come to think of it, Dad hadn't really left the house since the twins' funeral, and it was strange that he wasn't in his usual spot on the couch. But it was good that he had gone out. He needed to get out. Mom pushed the bathroom door open and we stared at my new hair in the mirror. Then she took me by the shoulders and turned me around. She searched my eyes for something— I don't know what—and then a smile cracked her face open.

"You're beautiful. You know that, right?"

I shrugged.

She kissed me on the forehead and smoothed strands of hair away from my eyes. "I'll see you in a couple hours. There's some leftover stir-fry in the fridge."

"Okay."

She tousled my hair. "It looks really good, Tamar."

"Thanks."

"Very natural."

"Good."

"Do you want to come to yoga tonight?"

"Nope."

"Sure?"

"Sure don't."

She sighed. "All righty, I'll see you in a bit."

"Yep."

I heard her close and lock the front door. She always did that when she left, but it had the disturbing effect of making me feel trapped inside the house. I unlocked the door and went to the fridge for a glass of milk. As I was pouring it, from the corner of my eye I saw some bushes moving in the backyard. I thought it might be a deer eating the new crocus shoots and went to investigate. I slid the glass door open and saw a ladder leaning up against the side of our house, and then I heard a low groan. I stepped outside and saw my dad lying on the ground. His right leg was twisted under him at a sickening angle. "DAD!" I ran to his side. "Are you okay? What happened?"

"I fell down." His eyes were bleary, and his skin was pea-green. There was a rip in his pants, and I could see the pale, jagged bone of his shin where it had burst through the skin of his leg. It glistened with droplets of blood and tissue. I turned away from him and vomited onto the grass. Then I ran inside to call 9-1-1. The dispatcher told me to put a blanket over him and wait with him until the ambulance got there, so that's what I did.

I was scared. I had never seen my dad hurt before. He mumbled a lot and wasn't making sense.

"When are they coming home?"

"Who?"

"The girls."

"Dad, it's okay. Just be quiet. You need to rest."

He grimaced and closed his eyes. "They're way past their curfew."

I sighed and tipped my head back. I saw two vultures floating in smooth circles miles above us.

"How long have you been like this, Dad?"

"Forty-two years."

The ambulance screamed up and two paramedics—one male, one female—hopped out and put Dad on an orange spine board and loaded him into the back of the ambulance. I was impressed by the speed and efficiency of their movements. There was something graceful about it, like an emergency-medical-team dance. They had him strapped in there in less than a minute.

"You're the daughter?" the female paramedic asked.

"Yeah."

"No one else home?" asked the male paramedic.

"No."

"Come with us, please." He held open the back door of the ambulance for me to climb in.

I sat beside Dad, and he reached for my hand. He kept asking questions, and the woman had to keep telling him to be quiet and take it easy. Finally, she put the oxygen mask over his face so he couldn't talk anymore. It was kind of funny because he hadn't said much of anything for months, and now that he was talking, he wasn't allowed to.

There was an amazing amount of equipment in the back of the ambulance, and as I looked around, I wondered if they had anything that could stimulate hair growth, like those electric-shock paddles or a shot of adrenaline or something. I didn't ask them, though, because I knew they had to focus on my dad. The paramedic asked me if I was okay. He gave me a bottle of water and a smile.

I called home from the waiting room and left a message for Mom on the answering machine. I didn't know the number of the yoga studio or even what it was called, so I couldn't reach her there. The parents and I didn't have cell phones because my mom thinks they give off radioactive waves and cause brain tumors. Maybe she'll change her mind after this. There was nothing she could do for Dad right now anyway. I wasn't even allowed in the room until the doctor was finished examining him.

I wandered around a bit and found the hospital chapel. I pulled open the heavy door. Candles flickered at the front of the room, and there were flower arrangements all over the stage. No one else was there, so I went in and sat down in one of the hard wooden pews. The air felt heavy and stale, but at least it was quiet. The solid oak doors blocked out the hospital beeps and buzzes, cries and shouts. I sat in the thick silence for a few minutes, then closed my eyes and bowed my head. I said a prayer for my dad. I prayed that he would be okay. I prayed that he wasn't paralyzed.

I prayed that he didn't have brain damage. I didn't know if I could handle it if he did.

I stayed there about fifteen minutes, and then my stomach started rumbling, and I left to find a vending machine. I had a bag of Cheetos and a Coke for dinner.

When I got back to the waiting room, Mom was sitting there, bouncing her knees up and down, clutching her purse in her hands. Her knuckles were white, and so was her face. She stood up when she saw me.

"Tamar! What happened? Is he okay?"

"I don't know. I think he fell off the roof."

"Oh for Christ's sake. What the hell was he doing on the roof?"

"Don't know."

"The hail," she said after a few seconds. "He was probably checking to see if it damaged the roof." She put her hand on her forehead, shook her head and rolled her eyes.

We waited together on the hard orange plastic chairs. I flipped through an old *National Geographic*, and my mom bounced her knees and clenched and unclenched her hands. Occasionally, she looked up at a TV that was playing the news. It was the same old: floods, fire and famine, pedophiles, perverts and freaks. Please, spare me.

Finally, the doctor came to get us.

"Mrs. Robinson?"

"Yes!" My mom jumped up and shook his hand.

"I'm Doctor Zwicky."

Doctor Zwicky was young and handsome, with jet-black hair that fell in a slant across his eyebrows. He looked like he belonged in an underwear commercial, not a hospital.

"How is he?" Mom asked.

"Well, he has a badly fractured tibia, a sprained ankle and a bruised tailbone. He also has a mild concussion, and he was severely dehydrated and in shock. But we're getting his fluids back up, and he seems to be through the worst of it. We've run some tests, and there is no sign of a fractured skull or brain damage. But we will need to keep him here for a few days."

My mom grabbed my hand and squeezed.

"Would you like to see him now?"

"Yes."

I hesitated, and my mom yanked me up by the arm.

"You can come too." Doctor Zwicky flashed me a smile that could save lives.

We followed his glowing white coat down the hall and into the elevator, up two floors and into room 308.

"Dad!"

"Hey T," he whispered. "Sheila." He smiled at Mom. His lips were cracked and white.

"David, what happened?" My mom reached for his hand.

"The hail completely destroyed our roof. We'll need to reshingle." His voice was scratchy, like he had laryngitis. His leg was in a cast already and was elevated by some kind of hook-and-pulley system. There were plastic tubes running from a bag of liquid into his arm.

He looked down at the mint-green sheet. "I don't know what happened. I'm sorry."

"Oh, honey. You didn't do anything wrong."

"Yes, I did. I fell."

We all laughed, even Doctor Zwicky.

"In six to eight weeks you'll be good as new, Mr. Robinson. But I'm afraid you'll have to get someone else to repair your roof."

Dad nodded, defeated.

"I'll give you a few minutes alone, and then I'll have to ask you to let our patient rest. He's had a very long day." Doctor Zwicky disappeared through the curtain.

I sat on the edge of the high hospital bed beside my Dad's good leg. I flipped some of my new hair behind my shoulder. "So, what do you think?"

"About what?"

I pointed to my head.

"Oh."

"Oh?"

"Glossy."

I smiled.

Mom told him she loved him and was glad he was okay. She kissed him on the forehead. "Get some rest. We'll see you tomorrow." She smoothed his face with the back of her hand, and his eyes fluttered closed.

We didn't say anything on the drive home. Maybe we were both too relieved to talk. I had a bath and went to bed, and my mom did the same.

From then on, I wore my wig all the time—except at night, when I kept it on its wig stand so it would keep its shape. If properly taken care of, a human-hair wig can last around twenty-five years. But I'm hoping (and praying) that my real hair will grow back way before then.

Dad came home after three days in the hospital. On Friday I got to stay home from school and help him, because Mom was at an all-day meditation intensive. Dad just watched TV and asked me to bring him his lunch and a few beers, and then he said it was a beautiful day and I had two good legs, so I should go for a bike ride. So I did. I found a sweet new single track in Fish Creek that was really challenging, and for a little while, I forgot all about being bald.

The next day, I wore my wig to go job hunting. I pulled it back into a ponytail because Mom said that looked more professional.

The first place I tried was Mik's Milk and Gas. I thought they were a good bet because the giant sign out front that posts the price of gas said *Now Hring*. I guess they ran out of *i*'s. I went inside, and the door beeped.

"Hi," I said to the lady behind the counter. Her marshmallow-colored hair was cut as if someone had placed a bowl on her head.

"Hi."

"I'd like to work here."

She pursed her pale lips and then ducked behind the counter. "Fill out this application form." She threw a clipboard down on the counter. Her puffy skin was the color of ashes.

"Thanks." I went to the back of the store by the slushie machine, sat down at a round orange table and read the first line: *Thank you for your interest in Mik's Milk and Gas!*

I looked around. There was no one in the store, and terrible soft rock was crackling out of the speakers. It smelled like burnt coffee and wet mop. A man came in and the door beeped. Another person came in and it beeped again; it seemed to be getting louder. A bell chimed because someone had pulled in for gas. Another bell. Another beep. I got up and went back to the counter. Miss Marshmallow was arranging cigarette packs on the shelf. Her back was as wide as a doorway.

"Excuse me?"

She turned around.

"Do you have a pen?"

She rolled her eyes and unclipped the pen from her shirt pocket, threw it onto the counter and turned back to the wall of cigarettes.

"Thanks." I picked up the pen. It was yellow and said *Mik's Milk and Gas* in red writing, and there was a stupid-looking cat on it giving the thumbs-up. I took it back to the table and filled out the application as best as I could. But I had no Previous Work Experience, Previous Employer or Reason for Leaving Last Place of Employment, so I had to leave those parts blank. It was a bit of a catch-22: you can't get a job without work experience, and you can't get work experience without a job.

As I handed Miss Marshmallow my application, I smiled and said, "Hope to hear from you soon," just like I was supposed to.

She grunted and scratched her doughy face. I left then and wondered, If I did get a job there, would the chime on the door drive me insane?

The same day I also filled out applications at these places:

a video store
a coffee shop
a drugstore
a fast-food restaurant
a sit-down restaurant
a movie theater
a bookstore
a car wash
a shoe store
a clothing store
a gift shop
a grocery store

a florist
a bakery
a jewelry store
a record shop
a thrift store

It was a long day. But I figured the more applications I filled out, the better chance I had of getting something. Cast a wide net. I was hoping for either the movie theater or the record shop, but everybody wants those jobs, and their application piles were probably four feet tall.

Around five thirty, I walked into a cute little pie shop down a side street in Avenida. It was full of old fogeys drinking coffee and eating butter tarts. The man behind the counter was probably a hundred years old. He had a crown of wispy gray hair. I asked him if he needed any workers, and his milky-blue eyes twinkled.

"Can you start right now?" he croaked.

"Sure, I guess."

"Fantastic." He swung the counter door open for me to enter the kitchen and tossed me a crisp white apron.

I have a job. I have a job! I work in a pie shop!

He pointed me in the direction of the sink, where a towering stack of dishes teetered precariously on the countertop.

"You can start with those, and then, when you're finished, we can make some pies." He winked. Then he ambled back to the front to finish his coffee and gossip with the other blue-hairs.

The dirty dishes were not just cups, saucers, spoons and forks, although they were there too. There were baking pans, muffin pans, pie plates and soup pots. It looked as if a giant blackberry had exploded all over these dishes and hardened on. The sign above the sinks gave directions on what to do: one sink was for washing and rinsing, and one was for sanitizing with bleach. I began to fill the sinks, the bleach stinging my nostrils. I poked around, looking for gloves, but couldn't see any. The old man came back into the kitchen and set a timer.

"Um, do you have any gloves?"

"What?"

"Gloves?" I mimed putting on a pair of gloves.

"No, no, I never use gloves. You don't need them." He scooted back out to the front.

I sighed, rolled up my sleeves, plunged my arms into the sink and began to scrub my way through the mess of lava-encrusted dishes. The dishwater was super hot, and I began to sweat. Sweat rolled from my armpits down into the crooks of my elbows. I guess this is why they call it elbow grease, I thought. Sweat ran between my breasts and dripped from my forehead. The sink was beside the massive oven, and I kept getting hotter and hotter. My skin reddened and began to burn and prickle from the bleach and the heat. After about twenty minutes, I thought I was going to pass

out from heatstroke and went to look for a washroom, to
splash my face with cold water.

The first door I tried led me into a walk-in freezer.
I turned to leave but then decided that it would be okay
to stay in there for a minute and cool off. The metal door
sucked shut behind me. I breathed in the icy air and
watched the steam rise off my body. Almost instantly, I was
chilled. I pushed on the door, but it wouldn't open. There
was a big circular metal handle, and I threw my weight into
it. It depressed and then sprang back against my ribs, but
the door didn't budge. I stepped back and stared at the door.
There must be some kind of trick to opening it that I didn't
know. There were actually three handles: the circular one,
a small rectangular one that pulled up, and a horizontal bar.
I tried them all in different combinations. The door still
wouldn't open. I started to shiver. It was cold enough to
freeze the balls off a brass monkey, as they say. I kicked the
circular handle hard, and it sprang back. Well, this is humiliating, I thought. I would have to bang on the door until old
Milky-Eyes came to rescue me. I began pounding my fists
against the freezer door. "HEY!" I yelled. "I'M LOCKED IN
THE FREEZER!" I felt like an idiot, but I kept at it for a
few minutes. "HELLO?"

No one came.

Goose bumps had popped out all over my body. I wrapped
my arms around myself and blew into my hands to warm
up, then tried the handles again. Nothing. I looked around

the freezer for a tool to pry the door open with, or a fire alarm to pull, or something to get me the hell out of that cryonic chamber.

What I found were six dozen boxes of frozen cookie dough. I started with chocolate chip, then moved on to white chocolate–macadamia nut. After I'd eaten as much cookie dough as I could, I tried the steel door again. It didn't open. I tried kicking it again. It didn't open. My fingernails were blue, and my knees and thighs trembled with cold. I took a frozen bag of tomato soup and thwacked it against the door again and again, until the brick of soup was shattered into slushy red flakes. "HELP!" I yelled as loud as I could before I realized that the old man was probably deaf. I tried smashing a bucket of ice cream against the handles, against the door itself. It wouldn't fucking open. Then the single lightbulb above me flickered once, twice...and went out. I was locked inside a freezer in total darkness. No one knew where I was. Tears slid down my face and froze on my cheeks. A pathetic whimper escaped from my shivering lips, and I curled up under a shelf of frozen pie shells to die.

SIX

The next thing I remembered was old Milky-Eyes shaking me by the shoulders.

"Hey, what the hell are you doing in here, kid?"

"I got l-l-locked in. I c-c-couldn't get out," I said through chattering teeth.

"Well, come on, get up." He dragged me up and out of the freezer, put a winter coat over me and handed me a steaming cup of coffee. "Drink that." He was eyeing me suspiciously. "What were you doing in there?"

"I-I was l-l-looking for the w-w-washroom."

He pointed to a stool beside the oven. "Sit down there until you warm up. Then you can go."

I sidled up to the oven and curled my icy hands around the white coffee mug, absorbing the heat. After about ten or fifteen minutes, I was sufficiently thawed.

Milky-Eyes came back into the kitchen. "All right, go on, get outta here, kid."

"What about…"

"What?"

"Tomorrow."

His blue eyes spit out icy sparks. "You didn't even finish the dishes! You think I'm going to hire you? Forget it! Get out of here! And don't come back!"

Under my breath I damned him to suffer in eternal hell. Then I threw my coffee cup in the sink. I ripped off the puffy jacket and tossed it on the stool, grabbed my backpack and headed for the front door. He scurried after me, shaking his fist. "Don't ever set foot in here again, you little thief!"

I flipped him off as I stomped out the door.

When I got home, Mom was sitting at the kitchen table, hunched over a stack of bills.

"Hey, how did it go today?"

"Fine."

"Did you get a job?"

"Yes and no."

"You want to talk about it?"

"Nope."

"Okay. Are you hungry?"

"No. Where's Dad?"

"He's in the garage."

"Right."

"Where else would he be?" She rolled her eyes. "He practically lives in there."

"I guess he can't get too far with a broken leg."

"He can't even drive, T."

"Maybe that's for the best."

"Shh!" She winked at me. I let a little snicker slip out, and so did Mom.

"Tamar, honey, would you do me a favor?"

"What?"

"Would you rub my neck a little bit? I was practicing shoulder stand today and I think I cricked my neck. It's really sore. Just right here." She grabbed the knobby part at the base of her neck.

"All right."

"Ooh! Your hands are like ice! Is it cold out?"

"No."

"Well, you know what your grandma used to say: cold hands, warm heart."

"What if you have warm hands?"

"What? Oh, I don't know. That feels really good. Yes, that's the spot. Right there. Ooh. Ow. I should've used a bolster, I guess."

"Yoga is the new plague."

"I just did something I shouldn't have."

"Yeah, yoga twenty-four/seven."

"It's what I need right now, Tamar. I wish you would try it."

I switched on my documentary-announcer voice. "Sheila Robinson, yoga victim, reveals all in tonight's exposé, 'A Downward Dog Spiral.'"

She giggled. "Aw, T. I can always count on you for a laugh."

"You're welcome." I stopped rubbing her neck and put some water on to boil.

"Maybe you could be a massage therapist."

"I don't think so, Mom."

I made myself a big cup of hot chocolate, then went to bed and piled six blankets on top of me. I was still shivering as I fell asleep.

Monday came early, as it always does. I was nervous as hell about going to school with the wig on. What if people could tell? What if it fell off? How was I going to style it? I wished, and not for the last time, that Abby and Alia were around to help me. They were actually very stylish individuals. Very chic. Fashionistas, they would say. I decided to wear the wig loose with a dark-purple toque over top, so it would look pretty natural, pretty real. I used extra adhesive to make sure it would stay put. The parents assured me that it looked terrific, so I had to take their word for it.

Nobody at school said anything. Probably no one even noticed—except one person: Roy.

"Is that real?" he said when I met him at his locker at lunchtime.

"Shh, keep it down, will ya?"

"Sorry. But...is it?" he whispered.

"What do *you* think?"

He reached out as if he wanted to touch it but changed his mind and adjusted the strap on his backpack instead. "I think acupuncture is very powerful," he said.

"Definitely." I nodded.

"But it would probably take more than one treatment to get that result."

Damn. Thought I'd fooled him.

"Looks great anyway," he said. Then he looked at his shoes.

"Thanks."

"How did your audition go?"

"No idea. The cast list should be up now. Let's go see if I made the cut."

As we navigated through halls teeming with hungry students, I told myself I didn't care if I was in the play or not.

The list was taped to the door. I scanned it quickly and didn't see my name.

"Tamar—"

"It's no big deal. I don't care. I didn't really want to be in it anyway."

"What do you mean?"

"I mean, I don't care. I'm not upset that I didn't make it."

Then Roy pointed to the top line of print:

Auntie Em...........................*Tamar Robinson*

"Ah!" I said.

"Ah!" he said.

"I made it! I'm in the play!"

"You're Auntie Em!"

Then I hugged him. I couldn't help it. I gave him a huge bear hug, and he gave it right back. Then I jumped up and down like an idiot for a while.

"Congratulations!"

"Wow, I didn't think...I mean...I thought maybe, but wow. This is so...I don't know..."

"Great? Wonderful? Fantastic?"

"Yeah."

"Let's go celebrate. Dairy Queen sundaes, my treat."

Sitting in that stained Dairy Queen booth, reading the initials carved into the table, was fantastic.

S.M. + A.A. = TL 4-EVER!

S.M. IS A FAGGOT!

4:20 4-LIFE!

I was on cloud nine. I had glossy hair, I had a role in the spring play, and I was eating a chocolate sundae with Roy Lee. Things were looking up. Maybe I would survive this after all.

seven

Our first rehearsal was the next day after school. Everyone introduced themselves, and then we got our scripts and did a cold read-through. I couldn't believe that I had been chosen to play Auntie Em. My favorite line was *We all got to work out our own problems, Henry.* Which I say right after Dorothy does her rainbow bit. The girl chosen to play Dorothy was Beth Dewitt. Beth was in grade twelve and had blindingly blond hair that came almost to her ass. She was supershort, not even five feet. She wasn't especially pretty, but she had breasts the size of basketballs, which gave her a significant edge in the ongoing popularity contest that is high school. She didn't say anything to me at the rehearsal, but if looks could kill, I'd be deader than a doornail, whatever that is.

There were nineteen people in the cast. Almost all of them were strangers to me. I knew a few kids, but not many. Cole Benson, the Scarecrow, was in my English class. He was always getting kicked out of class for making inane comments, but once in awhile he said something so ridiculous that the whole class, including Ms. Sanderson, busted a gut laughing. So Cole wasn't a total waste of skin. He had short dark hair that was blond at the tips, and he usually spiked it up with gel, but I thought it looked better without it. They say that gel can make you go bald over time. When I had hair, I never used it. Cole was popular with the ladies and had about a dozen girlfriends a year. He was cute in the same way that a sloppy, slobbering puppy is cute.

Sharon Strombolopoulous, also known as Yeti, was playing the Wicked Witch of the West. Kids had called her Yeti for as long as I could remember. She had a massive head of thick black hair, hairy arms and the damning shadow of a dark mustache. I would kill for a mustache right now.

I also knew Marcy Mavis, who was playing Glinda, the Good Witch of the North. Marcy had fine, honey-blond hair that was naturally straight and probably never tangled and always looked freshly washed. Marcy was perfect for the role of Glinda because she really was supersweet and nice to everybody and never said or did anything that might hurt someone's feelings. She had that soft, sugary sort of voice that makes you want to gag. Marcy was almost too good to be true. That's why I didn't want to be her friend, even though she tried to buddy up with me a bit last year. I went to her house once. We drank lemonade and painted our nails, but she didn't have anything interesting to say. She was like a cupcake—sweet and pretty, but all fluff on the inside. I wanted to hate Marcy, but I couldn't. She was too nice.

And I knew Scott McKinnon, the gay guy who was playing the Tin Man. He didn't know me though. He had light brown hair that he wore in a crewcut, and he was what my sisters would call superfine. Always well dressed, tall, cheekbones that could cut glass. He looked more like an adult than the rest of us.

The line reading was kind of boring, but I guess you have to start somewhere. Ms. Jane was excited. You could tell because she kept leaping around the stage to stand close to whoever was reading, and she would smile at them and say, "Great, great, excellent." Her enthusiasm was contagious. "I want you to know that The Wizard of Oz tops the list of my favorite plays of all time, and I know that all of you are going to make this a fantastic production!"

She said that Dorothy's story was the exemplary hero's journey, but that we were all important on the journey; each one of us was necessary, and we should all be very proud of ourselves for taking on this challenge.

I was just glad I didn't have to kiss anyone in the play. Lisa Arseneault, the girl who played Juliet last year, ended up getting mono.

Having mono is terrible. I know because Abby got it when she was in grade eight and all she could do was lie in bed and watch game shows and soap operas for three months. Even though she wanted to go outside and actually wanted to go to school, she couldn't. If she even came downstairs to get a drink, she would have to lie down on the couch for half an hour to rest afterward. So the four of us constantly took drinks and meals and homework and books and movies and stuff up to her room instead. She was a real whiny pain in the ass and would make you go back downstairs if you forgot to put sugar in her tea, and she hardly ever said thank you or anything. But we all kept doing it anyway, because that's what families do. They look after each other.

Sometimes, when I got my allowance, I would buy her a treat, like nail polish or a *Seventeen* magazine, to cheer her up. Her friends didn't even come over to visit her. I guess they didn't want to catch mono. One day, I went into her room to bring her some Gatorade, and she was lying face down on the bed, crying into her pillow. Her staticky auburn hair was all over the place. I put the bottle of Gatorade on her bedside table and sat down on the carpet beside her bed. She put the pillow over her head.

"GO AWAY!" she yelled.

"What's wrong?"

She started crying even harder. "Hefferewonfinks-imafathlult!"

"What?"

She removed the pillow and turned over. "Everyone thinks I'm a fat slut."

"Oh...are you?"

She threw the pillow at me. "I'm a virgin, Tamar! Okay? I'm a freaking virgin. How can a virgin be a slut?"

"How can a virgin give birth?"

"Oh *god!* Just go to hell already. Get away from me."

"Because you have mono, that's why they think that?"

"Obviously."

"'Cause you get mono from kissing?"

"That's not the only way you can get it. There are other ways too. It's highly contagious. It's probably the most contagious disease in the world."

"Right."

"What am I gonna do?" She flopped back on the bed, covering her face with her hands.

"I say screw 'em. Who cares what they think? They're probably just jealous because all the guys want to kiss you and not them."

"That's true."

"Well, forget about them then. They're idiots. You should be happy that you're so pretty and so many guys like you. I've never even kissed a guy."

"*Really?*"

"Nope."

"Tamar, you're, like, fourteen already!"

"So?"

"So you should already be way past your first kiss! What are you, gay or something?"

I shrugged.

"It's okay if you are. I mean, I won't disown you or anything, but holy crap, you need to get some action!"

"Why?"

"*Why?*"

"Yeah, why?"

"Because making out is fun! It's exciting!"

"I think it's gross."

"Well, you wouldn't know, would you?"

I shrugged again.

"You're gonna like it, trust me." Then she sat up and studied my face carefully, as if she was trying to figure out what was wrong with me. She looked at me for what felt like a long time, then squinted. "ALIA!" she yelled at the top of her lungs.

"She's not here."

"Where is she?"

"I don't know."

"How come nobody calls her a slut? You should see all the pathetic guys she goes out with. All these frigging loser skater boys that she meets at the punk shows. Frigging drug addicts."

"Well anyway, I wouldn't worry about what they're saying. People are morons. You know that."

"I guess. It really pisses me off though, you know? I feel like punching someone!"

"Take it easy, Abby. You should be resting."

"Rest, rest, rest! I'm sick and tired of resting! I don't want to rest anymore! I want to go outside and go to the mall and go to the movies and—"

"You'll be better soon."

"When?"

"Maybe next week."

"Promise?"

"I promise you're going to get better soon. You'll be making out again in no time." I stood up to leave.

"Tamar?"

"What?"

"Do you want to watch 90210 with me?"

"I can't. I have a ton of homework."

"Please?"

How could I say no? She was my sister, and she needed me. I sat on the end of her bed and we watched *Beverly Hills 90210* together. Abby fell asleep about twenty minutes into it, but I stayed and watched the rest, because I didn't want her to wake up and realize I had left her.

No one in our house caught mono from her, so maybe it wasn't the most contagious disease in the world. It was good that Alia had her own room, though, or else she probably would have caught it.

She and Abby were born identical, but they looked less and less alike as they got older. They had totally different clothing styles, haircuts, attitudes—everything. Alia was a punk princess, Abby was a pop princess. But they were each other's best friend forever. There was never any doubt about that. They even had their own special language. Silly words and phrases that didn't mean anything to anyone else but the two of them. And sometimes I wonder, That night as they lay dying, bleeding all over the road, what did they say to each other? Did they use their last breaths to offer each other some small comfort? I hope so. And I hope whatever they said was nicer than what I last said to the two of them.

To Abby, it was something like "Tarty. Now get out of my room" when she asked me how she looked. And to Alia, I was cold.

"Can I borrow your black belt, Tamar?"

"No."

"Why not?"

"'Cause you'll wreck it."

"I won't wreck it!"

"What do you even need a belt for? Your jeans are too tight already, Al. They're not gonna fall down."

"I need a black accent, okay?"

"Don't you have a black belt?"

"Only in karate! Hi-YAA!" She kicked the air between us and chopped it up with her hands.

I stared at her without smiling, which was an effort.

"Okay, I do have a black belt, but it's too wide for these loops. Please, Tamar? I will never ask you for anything ever again. I promise."

"I doubt that."

"Cross my heart and hope to die."

I rolled my eyes.

She put her palms together in front of her heart and made whimpering puppy sounds.

"Here." I opened my closet and threw the belt at her. "Now leave me alone. I'm trying to find the angle of this hypotenuse."

"Sure thing, Ms. Brainiac." She saluted me on her way out the door.

If I had known these would be the last times I would see either of them alive, what would I have said?

I'm sorry I wasn't the big sister you ordered. I'm sorry things between us weren't better. I wanted them to be. I never stopped loving you. I never stopped hoping things would change.

You think you have so much time. When you're sixteen, you think you have all the time in the world. But you don't, and you never know when your time will run out. I know I should have tried harder to be patient, to be kind. But it got to the point where I couldn't stand either one of them and could scarcely believe we were related.

Regret is like a heavy stone you carry around in your pocket. You know that it's useless. You know that it's weighing you down. But you just can't seem to throw it away.

eight

When I had told the parents that I would be playing Auntie Em in *The Wizard of Oz*. Their reaction wasn't quite what I had hoped for.

"That's wonderful, honey. When is the play?" Mom asked.

"Congrats," Dad said.

No high fives. No hugs. No whoops of joy. No champagne. No taking me out for dinner to celebrate. There was none of the enthusiasm and zeal I had imagined. Maybe they just didn't care. I know, I know, there are extenuating circumstances. But the twins are gone. I'm still alive.

When I opened my locker the next morning, a note fell out of the door. In big red bubble letters it said: *YOU ARE*

WAY TOO UGLY AND STUPID FOR ROY. STAY AWAY FROM HIM. I felt a sudden and severe seizing in my chest. I looked around. Everyone was acting normal. Chattering, laughing, zipping and unzipping backpacks. Everyone looked like they belonged there. No one was looking at me. I felt a wave of nausea well up from my guts. All the sounds of the hallway became muffled, and my vision blurred. I slid against the lockers and the floor rose up to meet me. I was dizzy. There was a weird *swish-swish* noise inside my head. Maybe I should start eating breakfast, I thought.

I turned the note over and over in my hands. It was an awful, awful message. Who would write that? It was on the same lined paper that everyone used. There were no other marks on the page. It had been ripped out of a three-ring binder and folded in half, twice. I didn't know what to make of it. I had never gotten a note before. Maybe the person who wrote it had slipped it into the wrong locker. Maybe it was meant for someone else. Maybe it was a joke. Or maybe...maybe someone was supremely and utterly jealous...of me. I didn't know what to do with the note and I didn't want to keep it, so I stuffed it into the recycling bin on my way to math class. I decided to try and block it out of my mind. But I had a little cry in the girls' washroom after math. I couldn't help it. It was just so *hateful*. I didn't do anything to anyone! I didn't do anything wrong. Roy was my friend! Why would someone give me that note? There are truly awful people in this world.

I didn't tell Roy or anyone else about the note. I was trying to learn my lines for the play, keep my grades up, keep my wig on *and* keep my parents from going insane. I didn't need this right now. I hated whoever had written it for making me waste so much time thinking about it. Asshole.

When I got home from school there was a message on the answering machine from Cruisy Chicken, a fast-food restaurant I had applied to. It was the manager, Don, asking if I could come in for an interview on Friday at four o'clock.

I was thrilled. I had an interview, and maybe soon I would have a paying job. But I couldn't go in on Friday at four because I had rehearsal. Dammit. Maybe I should skip the rehearsal. But I couldn't. Ms. Jane had said that if we missed two rehearsals without a doctor's note, we were out of the play. I looked up Cruisy Chicken in the phone book and dialed the number.

"Cruisy Chicken, how do you cockadoodle do?"

"Hi. Um…good. Can I speak with Don, please?"

"Can you hold?"

When Don came on the line, I told him I'd like to come in for an interview but wouldn't be able to make it on Friday.

"No problem. How about next Tuesday?"

"Um, that's not good either. I'm in the school play, and we have rehearsals most afternoons."

"I see. So when were you planning on working?"

"Weekends?"

"Only two days a week?"

"Yes?"

He sighed into the phone. "Well, then, just call me the next time you *can* make it in and we'll see if we can work something out."

At chess club the next day, I told Roy I had an interview at Cruisy Chicken.

"Wow, you're lucky."

"I am?"

Roy's parents wouldn't let him get a job, because they wanted him to concentrate on school. He had already sent out applications to University of Calgary, University of Lethbridge and University of Toronto, and as soon as he got his marks back from this term, he would apply to the University of British Columbia and Simon Fraser University. He wanted to study engineering. I don't know what kind of engineering. And I'm not sure Roy knows either. Roy is an only child. He has a lot of pressure on him to excel. I'm now an only child too, but it isn't the same only-ness as Roy's.

"You know that we are liv-ing in a ma-ter-i-al world and I am a ma-ter-i-al girl..." I caught myself singing in the shower

and instantly felt guilty because the parents were home and could probably hear me. But what's so terrible about singing in the shower, really? Still, I stopped singing and rubbed soap over my hairless head.

I scrubbed my scalp every morning with a loofah, hoping the exfoliation would open up the hair follicles and increase circulation, thus encouraging the hair to grow back. So far, there had been no new growth. Anywhere. I hummed quietly. Somehow, singing was no longer appropriate in our house. I wondered if the three of us would ever get over the death of the twins, or if we were condemned to be sad and un-singing for the rest of our lives.

I left for school earlier than I needed to, just to get out of the house. The sun was rising over the city, and when I looked up, my breath caught in my throat. It looked like the sky was on fire. The entire sky was blood red, leaking out fuchsia at the edges. A pale orange line scored the horizon. A chinook was coming.

The school day went by in a blur, and I retained nothing. Ms. Jane let me leave rehearsal early because I told her I had an interview. I had called ahead to make sure Don was going to be at Cruisy Chicken. I sat on a white plastic lawn chair in his office. He had mud-brown hair and the onset of male-pattern baldness. His forehead was sweaty, and he looked like he ate a lot of chicken. He hardly looked at my face; his gaze was concentrated on my chest. I don't know why. There's nothing to see there.

"What would you say are your three best qualities, Tamara?"

"It's Tamar."

"Tamar-ah?"

"No *ah*. Just Tamar."

He looked down at my application, confusion knotting his brow. "T-a-m-a-r. Tamar. Ah, okay, *Tamar*. Mind if I call you Tammy?"

"Uhhh…" I detested the name.

He ran a meaty palm over his face and through his thinning hair. "So, Tam, what would you say are your three greatest strengths?"

"Um, honesty. Integrity. And…stick-to-itiveness."

"Okay, great. And what about weaknesses?"

"Weaknesses?"

"Areas for improvement."

"I guess I can be too blunt, too direct, and sometimes that hurts people's feelings."

"Okay, anything else?"

"Um…"

"Areas for improvement."

"Yeah, I'm thinking."

He rapped his pen against his desk while I scraped my brain for something that wouldn't make me sound pathetic and unemployable.

"I'm not very…sociable."

"Oh." He squinted. "How do you feel about working as part of a team?"

"Fine."

"And you can work weekends only?"

"Right."

"Do you have reliable transportation?"

"The bus."

"Right. Well, do you want to try a shift Saturday and see how it goes?"

"As in tomorrow?"

"Yes. Saturday. Tomorrow. You want to work tomorrow?"

"Sure."

"Super." We shook hands and he squeezed my hand hard, finally looking me in the eye. He turned to the shelf behind him. "Here's your uniform. It will come off your first paycheck." He handed me a horrid red visor with a yellow cartoon chicken on it, giving the thumbs-up. I also got a red-and-yellow-striped golf shirt and a nametag that said *TRAINEE*.

I could barely hide my disgust. "And what did you say the starting wage was?"

"How old are you?"

"Sixteen."

"And this is your first job?"

"Yes."

"Five forty an hour. Welcome to the workforce." He pawed my shoulder as I turned to leave.

"Thanks." I looked at the other workers as I walked out. Everyone was running around, wrapping up chicken, shoveling fries into bags, yelling into headsets, shaking out fryer baskets. No one looked happy. And the place reeked. When I was out on the street, I brought a piece of wig hair to my nose and smelled it. It smelled like a grease trap already, and I had only been in there for twenty minutes. This was going to be a problem. I was only supposed to wash the wig once a week, max.

I got on the bus and hoped there would be a message for me on the answering machine from the manager of the video store.

But there wasn't. Just my dad propped up on the couch, cutting up beer cans with an X-Acto knife and listening to Maury Povich admonish gangster mothers.

"Dad, guess what?"

"Chicken butt?"

"Well, yeah. Sort of."

"What?"

"I got a job! I start tomorrow!"

"Where?"

"Cruisy Chicken!"

"Do you get free chicken?"

"I don't know."

"Well, you should work that into your contract."

"Okay…"

"So, that's good. This is your first job, right?"

"Yeah."

"Well, don't make it your last." And then he turned back to his mountain of mutilated beer cans.

I was too tired to ask what the hell he was doing with the cans. I went upstairs and studied my lines for the play. I wished that my sisters had been there to read for the other parts. The three of us could have acted out all the characters. That would have been a riot.

"TAMAR! PHONE!" My mom was home from yoga.

I went to the parents' room and picked it up. "Got it. Hello?"

Mom listened in for a minute and then hung up.

"Hey, Tamar, it's Roy."

"Oh, hey. What's going on?"

"My cousin and his girlfriend are coming in tomorrow from Lethbridge."

"Okay…"

"Yeah. So anyway, we're going glow bowling."

I said nothing. I saw the horrible note again in my mind.

"You know that one on the Deerfoot?"

"Um…"

"Well, would you like to come with us?"

"Bowling?"

"Glow bowling, yeah."

"Uh…"

"My cousin will drive."

"Ah, what the hell," I said. "Sure, I'll come."

"Cool. We'll pick you up around eight."

I hung up and went downstairs. Mom was making broccoli salad, and Dad was getting a beer from the fridge.

"Is it okay if I go to the Glow Bowl tomorrow night?"

"With who?" she said.

"What's that?" he said.

"Roy and his cousins. Glow-in-the-dark bowling."

"Is Roy your boyfriend?" Mom asked.

"No! Ew!"

"I'm just asking. It's okay if he is."

"We're not. He's not. He's just a friend who happens to be a boy, okay?"

"Okay."

"So, can I?"

"I don't see why not. David?"

"Who's driving?"

"Roy's cousin."

"How old is he?"

"I don't know. Twenty!"

My dad grunted.

"As long as you make sure to call us when you get there and let us know you're okay, and call before you leave and let us know when you'll be home," Mom said.

"And be home before ten!" Dad said. He hobbled back to the living room, waving a crutch for emphasis.

"Fine," I sighed.

This is what I will have to deal with for the rest of my life: paranoid parents, crazy early curfews, no driving with anyone under twenty years old and constant interrogation. All because my stupid sisters had to go and die. Frigging idiots.

Don't think that. Don't think that. God. I took a deep breath and held it in. Then, right before my lungs exploded, I slowly, slowly let it out. I went into the living room and gingerly readjusted Dad's leg so that I could sit on the couch with him while he watched the news and cut up cans.

"Dad, what are you doing?"

"Dr. Zwicky said I needed a project."

"So you're cutting up beer cans?"

"Yeah."

"That's...interesting."

"It keeps my mind off the pain."

"In more than one way..."

He chuckled. It was a rare sound from him lately.

"Two birds with one can, eh?" I said, kicking a can over to his side of the couch.

"Shh!"

"What?"

"What's that noise?"

"What noise?"

"Shh, listen."

"I don't hear anything."

He clicked the TV off.

A humming sound was coming from upstairs, directly above us. It would stop, then repeat, stop, then repeat, again and again. I closed my eyes and listened for a moment. It was strangely soothing. I opened my eyes and looked at my dad.

"It's your mother. She's doing that yoga chanting thing again." He reached into the cooler he kept beside the couch, cracked another beer and switched the TV back on.

That night I prayed. I prayed that all of my hair would grow back. I prayed that working at Cruisy Chicken would be okay. I prayed that my mom and dad would be okay. It took a long, long time for me to fall asleep. The sky had already begun to lighten when I finally drifted off, and I worried that I would sleep through my alarm and be late for my first real day of work.

Mom dropped me off at Cruisy Chicken the next morning.

"Good luck, Tamar. It's a proud day." She smoothed some of the hairs of my wig. She was getting all gushy over the fact that I had my "first real job."

"Don't get too excited, Mom. Besides, it's not a *real* job. It's a McJob."

"Well, you're going to do great." She leaned over and gave me a kiss on the cheek.

"Thanks." I hopped out, slammed the car door and hoped she wouldn't honk as she pulled out of the parking lot.

She honked.

I worked from 11:00 AM to 7:00 PM. I bagged fries and chicken and buns for eight hours. My skin was radiating chicken grease by noon. Only one person was nice to me. A guy named Mike, who said he was in grade ten at my school. I had never seen him before. He showed me how to close the tinfoil dishes faster by running a plastic knife along the edges. He told me we got free soft drinks during our shifts.

Don didn't work on weekends, and I was glad he wasn't there. The assistant manager's name was Karen. She had bleached-blond hair that she wore in a high ponytail. Her roots were coming in and had formed a dark crown around her hairline. On my fifteen-minute break I walked across the plaza to get some fresh air. I felt like throwing up. All I could smell was grease. A thick film of grease sat heavily on my skin, and I tried to scrape it off my face with my fingernails.

I could see the lights from the movie theater flashing around in the sky above me like the Bat-signal, and I wished I was working there instead. At the end of my shift, Karen asked if I could work the same hours the next day.

"Sure," I said. But I'd rather stab myself in the eye with a fork, I thought.

Mom was waiting in the car for me when I came out. "How was it?"

"Fine," I said.

"Did you bring any chicken home for dinner?"

"No. I never want to eat chicken again."

She laughed. "Your dad likes chicken."

"I'll bring him some tomorrow then."

When I got home, I threw my wig in the sink to soak the grease out of it. Then I realized I wouldn't have time to comb and dry it before Roy came to pick me up. I would have to wear a bandana. I had a shower and tried to erase the static blare of a hundred thousand orders for different Cruisy Combos rattling around in my head.

The doorbell chimed around quarter after eight. All three of us froze. No one had rung our doorbell in a long time, and it sounded hollow, eerie.

I slid across the hardwood floor and flung open the door.

"Hi," Roy said.

"Hi." I grabbed my coat and purse as the parents crept toward the doorway. "Mom, Dad, this is Roy."

"Hi, Mr. and Mrs. Robinson."

"Pleased to meet you, Roy," Mom said, smiling like he'd told her he'd discovered the cure for cancer.

Dad nodded, narrowing his eyes.

"What about your dinner, Tamar?" Mom said as I turned to go.

"I'll grab something at the bowling alley."

"All right. Take good care of her, okay, Roy?" Then my mom enveloped me in a huge hug, as if I would be gone for a year or something. She never failed to embarrass me.

"Sure thing," Roy said.

"Let's go. Bye!" We ran through the falling snow out to his cousin's car, a black Volkswagen bug. Roy and I were crammed in the back, and Roy's cousin, Lenny, and his girlfriend, Miranda, were sitting pretty up front. Lenny wore a gray toque; Miranda had black hair with bright red streaks that cascaded over her shoulders. I was exceedingly, wildly jealous of her hair. She looked like she belonged in a music video. Just looking at her hair made my innards ache with longing.

Miranda was a hairdresser at one of the upscale salons downtown, and Lenny was studying biochemistry at the University of Lethbridge.

"What are you gonna do after high school, Tamar?" Lenny asked as he merged onto the Deerfoot Trail.

"I'm not really sure. I mean, I don't...I haven't put much thought into it."

"Oh."

An awkward silence filled the little car.

"A paramedic, maybe." I was surprised as shit to hear myself say that. I hadn't even thought about it before that very moment. "Helping people through their emergencies, you know."

"That's brave work." He studied me in the rearview mirror.

"I could never do that," Miranda said. "Too much blood." She squirmed in her seat. "Oh, can we go to Peter's Drive-In? I *love* the food there! Can we, Len? Please? *Please?*"

"No sweat, my pet," he said. They made me want to barf.

The three of them ordered burgers and fries. I got a chocolate shake. The smell of the fries made me want to barf too, because I had been swimming in fry grease all day.

When we got to the bowling alley, we got lane number seven—my lucky number. It was really cool under the black light. Glowing stars and planets and aliens and spaceships floated on the walls and ceiling around us. Everything white looked ultraviolet. Especially people's teeth. Miranda ordered a Mike's Hard Lemonade and Lenny ordered a Heineken. Roy got a gin and tonic.

"For yourself?" the short blond server asked me.

"Um, I'll have a lemonade too, I guess." What the hell, I thought. You only live once, and they never ask for ID at bowling alleys. I excused myself and went to the pay phone to call the parents.

"Hello?"

"I'm here. Everything's fine."

"Tamar! Thank God." I heard her cover the mouthpiece and yell, "SHE'S OKAY!" before saying, "Your father was having a panic attack because you took so long to call. He thought—"

"We went to Peter's Drive-In first for burgers."

"Well, you should have told us."

"*Mom!*"

"What?"

"You gotta relax."

She breathed into the phone.

"I have to go. It's my turn to bowl."

"Okay, have fun, sweetheart. Have *fun*. Call before you leave. And be *safe*."

"Bye."

I went back to lane seven and took a big gulp of my hard lemonade. It was good.

"That's pretty awesome." I pointed to Roy's gin and tonic. It glowed bright purple under the black light.

"I know. It makes it taste better too." He laughed. "Want a sip?"

"Sure."

I didn't totally suck at bowling—I even got a few strikes. I enjoyed the feeling of getting a strike, the sound of the ball hurtling down the lane and the pins smashing into each other. I liked the weight of the smooth glowing ball in my hand, and the way the machine gently placed the pins back in perfect order each time they fell. Lenny and Miranda were actually pretty funny, in a cheesy sort of way. He would pat her bum encouragingly when she got a gutter ball and say, "Next time, peaches." And when she got a strike, which only happened once, she got so excited that she leapt into his arms and wrapped her legs around him, and they both howled with joy. Roy gave me high fives every time either of us got a strike.

I caught myself laughing a lot, even though I was trying not to smile with my mouth open because the black light made everyone's teeth look freaky and gross. It was fun. It was good to be out with people. To not think about my hair, my sisters, the parents, that awful note. To just pretend to be normal for a night.

When Lenny pulled into my driveway, Roy jumped out of the car. "I'll walk you to your door," he said.

I saw Lenny shoot him the thumbs-up.

We stood facing each other on my doorstep; bits of snow sparkled under the beam of the porch light. "Thanks for inviting me tonight," I said. "I had a lot of fun."

"Me too."

I stared down at Roy's checkered sneakers. My heart was squirming in my chest. Then he pulled me into him. We hugged for a long time, my face pressed against his collarbone. He smelled like snowflakes. Then he stepped back and moved his face in toward mine, but I turned my head quick and ducked inside. "Bye!" I said as I closed the door.

"Goodni—"

The parents were waiting up for me. Mom pretended to be watering a plant by the door, like she hadn't just been peeking out the front window. Dad was propped on the couch, drinking beer and cracking nuts open with a nutcracker.

"How was bowling?" Mom asked.

"Fine."

"Did you have fun?" Dad asked.

"Yep. Goodnight." Then I ran upstairs to my room.

What the hell was wrong with me? Why didn't I kiss him? I must be developmentally disabled. I stared at my reflection in the mirror and gave myself a stage slap upside the head like people do in the movies when they've done something totally idiotic. Then I got ready for bed and fell asleep thinking about what it would be like when I finally got up the nerve to make my first kiss happen.

I went to work the next day with a better attitude. I'd decided to accept my fate as a Cruisy Chicken employee. At least I would be making money and wouldn't have to rely on the parents for everything. At least I could bring Dad home some chicken, and maybe that would cheer him up a bit. At least I had gotten one call back from all those stupid job applications I had filled out.

It was busy, and I didn't even get to go to the washroom until my break. I guess no one wants to make dinner on Sundays because it's supposed to be a day of rest or something. Mike wasn't there and no one really talked to me except to yell orders at me. I noticed that all the workers had mild to severe acne. Excessively oily skin must be a workplace hazard. Well, that was something to look forward to.

I brought Dad home two drumsticks, a couple of wings and a bag of fries. I had to wash my wig again as soon as I got home because it had absorbed all the smells and oils from a thousand frying chicken parts.

That night the parents and I had dinner together at the kitchen table, which we hadn't done in a long time. Dad ate the chicken and Mom picked at the fries and I ate some spinach salad.

"David, Tamar," Mom said, her palms together, "I want to tell you something important."

We looked at her as we chewed our food under the harsh light of the fluorescent kitchen bulb.

"I've been accepted to go study yoga and meditation at a retreat center on an island in British Columbia."

Dad and I stopped eating.

"Stellar's Island."

We stared at her, unable to swallow the food still sitting in our mouths.

"I'll be leaving on Friday and I'll be away for six weeks."

Dad crushed his napkin and threw it on top of his plate. He scraped his chair back from the table and dragged himself to the garbage can on his crutches. He dumped the chicken bones and let his plate clatter into the sink.

I stared at her, unbelieving. She sat with her hands in her lap and a look on her face that I can only describe as hopeful. I looked at my dad. He stood in front of the sink, staring out the window into the dark, cold night.

The room was silent except for the metallic tick of the clock on the wall. Then my mother cleared her throat delicately.

"Are you serious?" I said.

"I am."

"How can you leave us now? With everything..."

She looked over her shoulder at my dad. "I know it's hard for you to understand, but I really think it's best for all of us that I take this time for myself right now, to walk my own path to healing."

"Dad's a freaking invalid right now. You can't leave."

"You'll be here."

"*What?* Why are you even doing this?"

"Because I don't know what else to do." She sighed and ran her hand through her hair. "I need a change of perspective. I just want to feel like myself again. And I think this will help me get there. I really do."

"You know we can't afford this, Sheila," Dad said.

"That's the great thing—it's a work-trade program. They grow all their own organic food and raise animals, too. Goats, cows, chickens, llamas, rabbits. I'll be helping in the gardens, mostly. It's community living. It's called The Yoga Farm."

A coarse, dry laugh came from my dad.

"*Jesus.* Are you sure it's not a cult?" I said.

"Look, I realize you guys must think I'm really selfish for doing this—"

"Yep," I said.

"But I've been trying so hard to get it together, so we can all get back to normal—"

"Mom, this *is* the new normal."

Dad turned the kitchen tap on and stared at the water rushing down the drain.

Mom put her head in her hands, and her shoulders shook with sobs. "I just don't know what else to do. I have to try. I have to at least *try*."

"What about—"

"I've left you a ton of lasagnas, casseroles and other goodies in the deep freeze."

I stared at her.

She wiped the tears from her face. "It's only forty-two days!"

"What about me, Mom?"

"You're doing *fine*, honey. You're doing better than all of us. You have a new job, you have a nice boyfriend—"

"He's not—"

"You're in the school play, your grades are excellent. Look at you. You don't need me."

"Yes. I. Do."

"I'll be back in time to see you in your play."

I folded my arms on the table, put my head down on them and closed my eyes. A commune? Was this a joke?

She came over to me and rubbed her hand in small circles over my back. "Don't cry, Tamar. Please don't cry."

"Why not? Everyone else is."

She walked to the sink and stood beside my dad. She turned off the tap and looked up at him. "I'm sorry, David, but I need to do this. I really do. I didn't tell you before because I didn't think I would be accepted into the program, and then your leg..." She reached for his hand, and he pulled it away. They stood motionless with their backs to me. Inside, I felt hollow and cold. I quietly left the table and tiptoed up to my room. I crawled into bed and squeezed my eyes shut as tight as I could. The tears came anyway.

nine

Friday came too fast. Mom said *goodbye* and *have fun* and *be good*, and she hugged and kissed us. Then she got into a taxi and left me alone with a crippled dad I barely recognized and certainly couldn't talk to. I still couldn't believe that she would leave us.

Dad and I stood on the front step in the frosty morning air and watched the cab roll away until we couldn't see its taillights anymore. Then we turned to each other, and I wondered if I looked as sad as he did. I gave him a hug.

We went inside and Dad hit a pile of his beer-can pieces with his crutch, and they flew across the living room. Squares and circles and ovals and rectangles and long thin strips of metal lay scattered across the carpet. Then he stretched out on the couch and closed his eyes as if he was in terrible pain. For a minute I watched him lie there, drowning in the quicksand of his own grief. Then I carefully stepped around the pieces and went into the kitchen. I scrambled three eggs and made four slices of toast. I divided everything between two plates and gave one to my dad. We ate on the couch together in silence.

I had decided to start eating breakfast.

As I walked to school through the gray, icy morning, it occurred to me that Mom might never come back. She might have just left us for good.

But no, she wouldn't do that.

She couldn't do that.

Could she?

I kept walking, trying not to slip on patches of black ice.

I was on my way to my first class, carrying my textbooks and binder, when—BANG!—somebody slammed into me, and I dropped everything and fell on the floor. My binder rings snapped open, and a hundred pages of notes fluttered through the hall. People trampled all over them, not caring. I rubbed my shoulder where I'd been smacked. I didn't see who had pushed me. No one said sorry. Nobody helped me up. It was going to be a long day.

The only good part of the day was rehearsal, where I got to pretend to be someone else for a few hours. And Friday was my favorite rehearsal day because we always stayed longer—it always felt like we got more done. The theater was so different than the rest of the school. The stage was black with black curtains, and the seats and floor were black too, so it felt like you were entering a secret cave. There were no windows. Somehow it made me feel safe.

Ms. Jane had us begin with some trust exercises.

"Light as a feather, stiff as a board." She clapped her hands. "In character! Auntie Em, you're up."

"I'm okay."

"Come on, let's go."

"No, really, I..."

"We won't drop you," said Cole. "Not on purpose anyway."

Everyone laughed. Even me. I lay down on the stage and crossed my arms over my chest. Tin Man and Lion kneeled on my left side, Scarecrow and the Wicked Witch of the West on my right. They each slipped two fingers of each hand beneath me and began to chant, "Light as a feather, stiff as a board. Light as a feather, stiff as a board." I trembled and closed my eyes. "Light as a feather, stiff as a board." I felt myself rise off the stage, but I couldn't feel their fingers anymore. My body felt suspended in the thickness of the air. I was floating. I was weightless. "Light as a feather, stiff as a board! LIGHT AS A FEATHER, STIFF AS A BOARD!" My eyes popped open. I was high above the stage, above their heads. I panicked and began to flail. The black stage rushed up to meet me. Before I crashed into it Scott caught me and set me gently on my feet.

"You all right, Auntie Em?" he said.

"Yes, yes, I believe I am." I brushed myself off and ran my hands over my wig to make sure it was still in place. My heart was racing.

"Good thing I was just oiled this morning, or I would never have been able to catch you." He smiled.

Beth Dewitt rolled her eyes and lay down between us to be lifted. "I'll show you losers how it's done," she hissed.

I don't know why they cast Yeti as the wicked witch; Beth would have been perfect for it.

When I got home, I found Dad on the couch in the exact same position he had been in when I left. Leg propped on three pillows, beer-can parts still strewn across the room. I wondered if he had moved at all during the day.

"What's up, Dad?"

"The ceiling."

"Good one."

He grunted.

"Need anything?"

"Yeah, a new roof."

"Oh yeah, the hailstorm."

"I didn't get the insurance that covers hail damage."

"Really?"

"Yeah." He looked down at his stained jogging pants.

"Shit."

"I thought if anything happened, I could just fix it myself. Save us the money."

"So…now what are you going to do?"

He slowly shook his head back and forth and continued to stare at the ceiling. I looked up. A hairline fissure unfurled above us like a baby vine, but I could swear it had always been there.

"I don't know," he said. "Beg, borrow or steal it. Hope it doesn't rain anytime soon."

"Well"—I patted him on the shoulder, trying to sound cheerful—"I think it'll be okay, Dad. The forecast calls for clear skies. Let me know if there's anything I can do to help."

"Can you bring me the phone and the phone book?"

"Sure." I walked into the kitchen.

"And another beer?"

After carefully inspecting the upstairs ceiling for cracks and leaks and finding neither, I went into my room, put on the radio and combed out my wig with the special wig comb. I took it off and felt my head for any new growth. Then I examined my legs and arms under a magnifying glass. Not a whisper of hair to be found anywhere. Smooth as a baby's ass.

I heard Abby's voice in my head. *"Hey, look on the bright side. At least you don't have to shave your legs anymore."*

I don't know what happens when you die. But once in awhile I get this strange feeling that my sisters are watching me from somewhere else, like another planet or something. And sometimes I hear them speak inside my head, clear as a bell. It's weird, I know. It's crazy.

After their accident I went to see a grief therapist, aka a shrink, a few times. I still had all my hair then. The grief therapist had short gray hair and looked like an elf. Her name was Nina. I couldn't stand Nina and her nasally questions and her surreptitious note-taking and her stinky vanilla perfume. Talking to her made me even more depressed about the whole double death situation, so I quit after three sessions.

She did get one thing right though: she said that life is a series of painful, tragic, unbearable events, and the best we can do is fumble through it with our chins up.

Nina wanted to load me up on antidepressants so I could be another placid zombie success story. I told her exactly where she could shove her antidepressants.

I rubbed some cream that I had bought at the drugstore into my head. It claimed to renew hair growth and had a man with an afro on the bottle. It smelled horrible and made my eyes sting. I sat down on my bed. There was a DVD on my pillow. I picked it up. On the cover was a beautiful blond woman in a hot-pink leotard. She was standing on one leg and had the other one wrapped around her ear. She was smiling as if she had just won a million bucks. The title said

Yoga for Happiness. I flipped the case over. On the back was a yellow Post-it note.

Tamar, I hope you will try this video. It could be just the thing you need. Please look after yourself. See you soon. Love you forever.

Mom

I looked at the woman on the cover again. I laughed. There was no way. There was just no way. I shoved the DVD into the back of my closet and decided to forget about it.

Just who did my mother think she was? Flaking off like this, abandoning us in our time of need? And for what? So she could sit under a gigantic tree in the middle of the Pacific Ocean and pick her nose with her toes? It was obscene.

I put on a toque and went downstairs. I ate a spoonful of peanut butter and then heated up a can of tomato soup and made two grilled-cheese sandwiches. I poured the soup into two bowls and put them and the sandwiches onto plates, with pickles on the side. I went to the living room, careful not to step on any of the scrap metal, and handed a plate to my dad. He looked right through me. He was watching a rerun of *Star Trek: The Next Generation.*

"Thanks." He started eating without even looking at his food.

I sat down at the end of the couch. "What's going on?"

"Did you know that Vulcans are incapable of experiencing emotion?"

"Yeah, they're the sociopaths of the universe."

"Wouldn't that be nice? To have all logic and no emotion?"

"I don't know."

"I think it would be great." He crunched down on his pickle, then took a swig of beer.

"Did you call the roofers?"

"Yeah, they'll be here Monday. "

"That's good."

"They'll let me pay it off in installments."

"Great."

"Yeah." He sighed and turned back to Captain Jean-Luc Picard, who I have to admit, was a man who wore his baldness well.

I had homework I should have been doing, but I decided to let my mind take a backseat and let the crew of the starship *Enterprise* drive.

I went to bed when *Letterman* came on, leaving my dad snoring on the couch, bathed in flickering blue light.

I dreamed that I was the captain of the *Enterprise* and we visited an alien planet that was bright purple with massive fluorescent-pink palm trees and a black ocean. All the aliens on the planet looked like Abby and Alia, but none of them had any hair. They were a violent, bald race. They tried to kill me and my crew with their mind-warping powers. They made our brains bleed. They reached through our rib cages into our chests and squished our hearts. We zapped them with our phasers and fled to the safety of our ship.

ten

On Monday in gym class, we were separated from the boys while they started their wrestling unit. The girls in our class were put with the grade-twelve girls to play basketball. Beth Dewitt, aka Demonic Dorothy, was on my team. She was a pretty decent player. Even though she was the shortest one in the gym, she was fast. But she kept fouling, and she didn't pass the ball to me once, even when I was wide open and standing under the net flapping my arms, yelling her name.

Afterward in the girls' change room, I overheard Lana Thompson telling Jess Kazinski that Beth was going to have to bind her breasts for the play because they were too big to fit into her Dorothy costume.

"Is that true?" I asked.

And then Beth was there. She stood in front of me with her hands on her hips while I tried to change covertly behind a locker door.

"Is what true?"

Jess and Lana said nothing. They closed their lockers and went to the mirror to redo their makeup.

"Tamar," Beth said loudly, "I asked you a question. What were you talking about? I heard my name."

"It's nothing," I stammered. "Never mind."

"Tell me!"

"Um…"

All the girls in the change room turned to look at us.

"You never do what you're told, do you?"

"I don't know…"

"Are you spreading rumors about me, Tamar?"

I looked at Jess and Lana for help. They were suddenly fascinated with their mascara.

"Because rumors can really hurt people." Beth looked at her friend Madison, who had come up behind me. Madison probably had fifty pounds on me. She had red hair and four fat brothers and was tough as a rusty nail. Madison sneered at me and smacked her fist into her palm.

"I…I don't…"

"Just apologize before we have to hurt you," Madison said.

"On your knees," Beth said.

I looked around the room. No one was going to help me; no one even cared.

"And I'll tell you another thing, Tamar. The only reason Ms. Jane gave you a part in the play is because she feels sorry for you because your slutty little sisters went and got themselves killed."

"Beth," someone near the showers said.

"Shut up. I'm talking now. You'd better get down on your knees and apologize to me right now or I swear to God I will make your life a living hell."

"Too late for that," I mumbled.

"What?"

"I don't want to," I said in a small voice.

"Look, Tamar. I'm doing you a favor. You need to learn a few things before you get to grade twelve. Like who gets respect and who has to bow down. You, and all the people like you, bow down." She laughed a horrible, high-pitched laugh, and some other girls laughed too. Then she leaned over and hissed, "You'll never be good enough for Roy, so don't even try."

I felt the blood burning my face scarlet, but I didn't care. My hands balled themselves into fists and trembled at my sides. I took a deep breath, held it in and started counting to ten.

"I'm waiting for my apology." She crossed her arms over her massive chest and twisted up her lips. She tapped her foot twice.

And then something inside me exploded.

I didn't even think about doing it. Something took over my body and made it move. I punched Beth Dewitt right

square in her little button nose. It immediately began to
ooze blood. She yelped and covered her face with her hands.
Some of the girls in the change room started chanting "Fight,
fight, fight" and formed a circle around us. Everything was
happening in slow motion. Beth slapped me across the
face, and I smacked her right back. "You ugly little bitch,"
she said. Then it was on. The girls chanted louder. "FIGHT,
FIGHT, FIGHT!" I elbowed Beth in the breasts and she hit me
in the ribs. I kneed her in the stomach and she kicked me in
the shins and punched me in the mouth. I dragged my fingernails across her face. She screamed and grabbed my throat.
I sacked her in the jaw and then she grabbed a chunk of my
hair. "Okay, okay, I'm sorry! I apologize!" I said, clawing at
her wrist. But it was too late. She ripped my wig off and there
I was, exposed, bald as a bowling ball, in front of everyone.
The girls stopped chanting. Everyone was silent. You could
have heard a tampon drop.

Then Beth laughed. Her laughter echoed off the
tile floor and walls and still echoes now in my mind.
"She's a freak!" she said, holding up my wig like a trophy.
"She's a fucking *freak!*" Then the other girls started saying
"Oh my god" and "Holy shit" or just gaping openly, for a
couple of minutes or a thousand years, while I stood there
with the metallic taste of blood filling my mouth, looking at
the floor, letting it all happen.

Eventually the bell rang, and everyone packed up their
bags and left as if nothing out of the ordinary had occurred.

Everyone but Beth, who still stood in front of me, staring. I closed my eyes and held out my hand. She let her breath out through her teeth and dropped the wig into my open palm. I heard her runners squeak as she turned away and pushed through the change-room door, laughing to herself. I opened my eyes a crack to be sure I was alone, and then I sank to the floor and wept. I cried so hard I threw up. I turned off the lights and curled up on one of the hard wooden benches. I stayed there all period and didn't even think about going to English class. At the beginning of the next period, my name was called over the PA with instructions to report to the principal's office. I splashed my face with water and dabbed at my bloody lip with a paper towel. I put my wig back on and looked in the mirror. I looked like shit. I pulled my sunglasses out of my purse and put them on, then walked slowly to the office.

Beth had told the principal that I lost it on her after gym class for no good reason. She had brought in witnesses to confirm that I had hit her first and that she only acted in self-defense.

"Is it true what Beth has told me, Tamar?" Mr. Ivers asked.

I stared at the flecks of blue and brown in the carpet as I sat slumped over in a chair beside Beth.

"Tamar?"

"Yeah," I muttered.

"You know that there is zero tolerance for violence at this school?"

"Yeah."

Mr. Ivers sighed. "Well, I'm sorry to have to do this, but school policy dictates that you must be suspended for no less than one week."

"Fine."

"That means you're not permitted on school property for any reason for seven days."

"What about for play rehearsal, after school hours?"

"Not for any reason."

I looked sideways at Beth. She sat up straight, looking smug, with her legs crossed and her humongous boobs jutting out the top of her sweater. I hated her.

"Fine."

"I hope you understand that this will go down on your permanent record."

I didn't say anything. I stared at the carpet and decided it was ugly.

"Now, I think you owe Beth an apology."

I couldn't believe it.

He cleared his throat and tapped a pen against his desk.

I turned to her. "Sorry," I said through clenched teeth.

She looked away.

"You're to gather your things now and leave school property. Your teachers will be informed of the reason for your absence, and any assignments or tests you miss this week must be made up when you return. I'll be phoning home and letting your parents know about the situation. You're both dismissed."

As I walked down the hall to my locker, I heard people whispering and saw them nodding toward me and staring and talking behind their hands.

They already knew.

Everyone already knew.

I might as well get on the PA and make an announcement: "Hello, Canyon Meadows High. This is Tamar Robinson speaking. Yes, the sister of the evil twins, now deceased. If you haven't already heard, I am actually completely bald. Not just on my head, but on my entire body. Yes, even down there. And I will probably be hairless for the rest of my life. Thank you for ostracizing me, and have a nice day."

I trudged home in a daze. The sun was way too bright, glittering off all the snow and burning into my retinas. The sky was a brilliant, piercing blue. A blue so pure and perfect it hurt to look at it.

I was sore all over. My whole body felt like it had been slapped, and I could feel my lips growing puffy and fat. I had an urge to stick my head in the snowbank, but I didn't.

I sighed as I stepped into the warmth of my house. It was quiet, without the TV blaring.

"Dad!"

No answer.

I peeked into the kitchen. He wasn't there. I realized this was the first time I had been alone in my house in a very long time. I closed my eyes and listened to the hum of the fridge. The sound reminded me of my mom doing her yoga chanting. I had a deep and sudden ache inside my chest. I leaned against the wall dividing the kitchen from the living room. Then my dad came through the garage door on his crutches. He reeked of cigarettes.

"Dad!"

"Hi, T. What happened there?" He pointed to my lip.

"I'm not ready to talk about that."

"Roger that."

I waited to see if he would say anything about Mr. Ivers calling. He didn't. I checked the answering machine. No messages. I went upstairs, changed my clothes and took off my wig. I put it on its stand, then shoved it to the back of my closet. What was the point of wearing it now that everyone knew I was bald? It would be posing. And I hated posers.

I went to the mirror and examined my face. My lip looked like a baseball glove and had flakes of dried blood on it. I felt around inside my mouth with my fingers. No teeth loose or missing—that was lucky. It could have been worse, I thought. *"No, it couldn't have,"* I heard Alia say in my head. I was glad my mom was gone, because I would have been too ashamed to tell her what had happened in the locker room that day.

I washed my face and brushed my teeth and put on my blue flannel pajamas. I pulled down my blinds, got into bed and closed my eyes. When I closed my eyes, I saw the girls' faces in the change room at the moment my wig had been ripped off. At first, their soft pink mouths had formed little Os of shock and surprise, and then they had contorted into such ugly shapes of vicious, scathing laughter that it was hard to believe any one of those girls had a kind heart. I tried to squeeze the whole savage scene out of my head, but it was there to stay, maybe forever.

I stayed in bed for the rest of the afternoon and all night. It had been the single-most humiliating day of my entire life, and I didn't want to come out until it was over.

eleven

I woke up in a sweaty panic in the soft gray light of dawn. I didn't know who I was or where I was. I looked down at myself. My blue pajama top fell across my body like a piece of the sky. I put my hands over my belly, tried to slow my breathing, my heart rate. And gradually I remembered that I was Tamar, I was at home in my bed, my sisters were dead, my mom was gone, my dad was crazy, and I was bald and the whole world knew it. I closed my eyes and willed myself back to sleep, because sometimes even bad dreams are better than real life.

When I got up hours later, I called Cruisy Chicken and told Don I could work any day that week if he needed me. Figured I might as well make some money if I wasn't going to school.

"Fantastic. Why don't you come in tomorrow at eleven?" he said.

I drank a glass of orange juice and stood in the kitchen, listening to the eerie quiet of the house around me. Dad wouldn't be up for another few hours, Mom was gone, and I was still getting used to not hearing the sounds of my sisters.

There was a blanket of new snow insulating everything. I could hear creaks and groans coming from the walls and the floors and the furnace, but other than that it was silent. First period would just be starting. My biology class would be taking a test on the parasympathetic nervous system. I was glad I wasn't at school. I wrapped the silence of the morning around me like a scarf. I made a cup of tea and drank it as I gazed outside.

The snow sparkled like a hundred billion diamonds piled up in our backyard. I put on my coat and slippers, slid the back door open and crunched down to the lawn.

When I found the right spot, I fell back into the snow and moved my arms and legs into the shape of an angel. It was something my sisters and I always used to do when there was a fresh snowfall. I stopped moving and lay still for a while. Snow fell noiselessly around me. I let the sun shine down in my face as I stared up at the white sky. I could almost smell the sky, that's how close it was. The snow beneath me was like a soft fluffy blanket; it felt cool against the bare skin of my head. I watched the crystalline clouds of my breath float away, and I blinked snowflakes out of my eyes. And then suddenly there was so much light, it was as if the world had cracked open. It got brighter and brighter, until I couldn't stand it anymore and had to close my eyes. But the light didn't go away. It was dazzling. I stayed absolutely still and tried to focus on the insides of my eyelids. My whole body got warm and I felt like I was melting into the snow. After a minute or two, I slowly opened one eye, then the other. Then I stood up carefully so as not to ruin my angel and stepped back to look at her. She was beautiful.

You would never be able to tell from a snow angel if someone was bald or not. I thought she looked a little lonely in the middle of all that stark white snow, so I made two other angels, one on either side of her. And as I was doing it, I was smiling.

But I stopped smiling when chunks of the sky were hurled down upon me. I yelled, throwing them off as if they were on fire, and jumped to my feet. Then I realized they weren't slabs of the sky at all—they were shingles. Our roof was being torn apart.

"Oh, sorry," said a tall man wearing a baseball cap, squinting down at me from the roof. "Didn't see you there."

I pulled my hood up over my head and went inside, banging the glass door closed behind me.

Roy called at 3:47 PM.

"Tamar, I heard what happened. Are you okay?"

"Yeah."

"I got your assignments. Do you want me to bring them over?"

"Um, sure. That would be fine."

"I'm on my way." He hung up.

I went upstairs and put on my purple toque. I wasn't wearing my wig anymore. I was mad at my wig. For not sticking to its adhesive. For letting Beth Dewitt rip it off me in front of thirty-six girls. My wig sucked shit. My wig was not worth $769 if it couldn't even stay on my head during a stupid fight. I put my false eyelashes on and carefully drew on my eyebrows. I put down the pencil and stared back at my reflection. I wasn't the ugliest person alive. *"You're a whole lot prettier than Beth Dewitt,"* I heard Abby say. *"Even without boobs."* And then Alia was singing, *"U.G.L.Y. She ain't got no alibi! She's ugly!"* I smiled into the mirror.

Roy arrived; his kaleidoscope eyes looked big and worried and beautiful. He gave me a hug, and I let myself be hugged. He smelled like fresh ginger.

"You okay?" he said in my ear.

"Yeah."

We kept hugging. I heard Dad turn the TV down so he could eavesdrop. We went into the kitchen and I put the kettle on for tea.

"Here's your work." Roy placed a small stack of papers on the table.

"Thanks."

"Oh, and Ms. Jane said it's okay that you have to miss this week of rehearsals because there are extenuating circumstances. She said they'll get someone to stand in for you."

I rolled my eyes. "Nice to know I'm so easily replaceable."

"You're not and you know it."

"Whatever."

"I can't believe Beth did that."

"Believe it."

"So, what are you gonna do?"

"What can I do?" I shrugged. "Life will go on, with or without my hair."

He nodded and bowed his head as I handed him a steaming cup of green tea.

We sat there in silence for a minute, blowing on our tea.

"She should be kicked out of the play," Roy said.

"I don't know, maybe just a role change…she'd make a pretty mean Munchkin."

Then Roy started laughing and so did I, and we sat there at my kitchen table laughing and laughing until tears rolled down our cheeks and fell into our tea.

The next morning I took the bus to Cruisy Chicken. I wore a black bandana, no wig. If anyone noticed, they didn't say anything. Don sat in his office on the computer all day, probably looking at greasy porn. Mike started at 3:45 PM, and I was glad when he got there. I didn't know if he had heard about the fight and my wig and everything, but if he had, he didn't seem to care. We made fun of customers and made up dead-baby jokes together.

"What do you call a dead baby, a rat, a six-week-old bun and a pickle?"

"What?"

"Cruisy Combo number three, hold the fries."

"What do you get when you put a dead baby and a cup of Tabasco in the blender?"

"What?"

"Cruisy's secret sauce."

"Why did the dead baby cross the road?"

"Why?"

"Because it was stapled to the chicken."

We doubled over with laughter.

"Okay, what am I? What am I?" Mike turned away from me and then spun back around hissing, two french fries stuck up his nose and his eyeballs rolled back in his head.

"An epileptic walrus!" I guessed.

"No! A dead baby that fell into the deep fryer!"

"Ohhhhh," I groaned.

"Thanks for playing. Here's your consolation prize!" He picked a fry out of his nostril and presented it to me.

I took it from him and held it up for the fake studio audience to see. Then Don walked out of his office. I pretended like I was just throwing the fry in the garbage and gave Mike, whose back was to Don, a warning look.

He got it and took the other fry out of his nose and put it back in a bag of fries.

"Order up!" Don barked.

I tried to keep a straight face while I bagged the order and took it to the window for a blond lady in a yellow Jeep. There was a fluffy white dog in the passenger seat, and I had a hunch the chicken was for him.

"Tam, step into my office."

Mike made a face behind Don's back like he'd just eaten something disgusting.

Once I was standing in Don's office, he closed the door and pulled out the plastic lawn chair for me.

"Have a seat, Tam."

When I was sitting, he placed his thick hands on my shoulders. He began massaging my shoulders, lightly at first, then harder.

I cleared my throat and squirmed a bit in the chair. He didn't stop.

"You like working here?"

"It's okay," I said.

"Yeah?" He pressed his thumbs deep into my upper back.

"Yeah."

He began to rub my neck, and then he ran his hands several times from my shoulders down the length of my arms to my wrists. "You're very tense," he whispered, his lips close to my earlobe.

"Um, I need to use the washroom." I stood up fast, nearly knocking the chair over.

Don sighed. "Here's your paycheck," he said, handing me a brown envelope from a stack on his desk.

"Thanks. Did you want me to work again tomorrow?"

"No, I think we'll be okay without you tomorrow."

When I came out of the office, Mike looked at me, searching my eyes, his face tight with concern. I shook my head and went into the staff washroom. I locked the door and sat on the toilet, feeling shaky and gross. A slimy layer of sweat had formed on my skin. I fought down the vomit that was threatening to erupt and ripped open the brown envelope. It was my first paycheck ever, and it was for seventy-two dollars and thirty-nine cents. Diddly-squat.

I hung my head in my hands. Hot tears stung my eyes. Then someone knocked on the door of the bathroom.

"Just a minute!"

"Are you okay?" It was Mike.

"Yep!" I lied.

I blew my nose and washed my face at the sink, then retied my bandana and prepared to face the disturbing world of chicken slinging once again.

When I came in the door, Dad looked up from his can cutting and turned the volume on the TV down.

"Hey, Dad."

"T."

"What's up?"

"Time's up."

"Not bad." I headed for the kitchen.

"Bring me a beer from the fridge?"

I unwrapped the chicken burger I had brought home for him and heated up the fries in the microwave. I made myself a peanut-butter-and-pickle sandwich and went back to the living room to eat with him.

"Thanks." He opened the can, twisted off the tab and placed it carefully on top of a pile of tabs beside the couch. "Want one?" He looked at me.

"Can I?"

"Sure, when you turn eighteen."

"*Dad!*"

He laughed. "Grab yourself a soda, kiddo." I took a ginger ale from the fridge, then went back to the couch.

"So..." he said.

"So?"

"Cheers." We clinked cans and both took a swig, and it was good. "So, I got a phone call from Mr. Ivers..."

"Oh yeah?"

"Were you going to tell me about that?"

"There's nothing to tell."

"I see." He nodded, tilting the can to his lips.

I took a gulp of ginger ale and a bite of sandwich and then another big guzzle. I took a potato chip from the open bag on the floor, ate it, took another one, had another drink, sighed. Then I told him the whole damn thing. But I left out the part where Beth called my sisters slutty because Dad didn't need to hear about that.

He listened quietly and nodded at certain parts. He didn't interrupt me to ask questions like my mom would have. When I was finished, he said, "Well, I can't blame you."

"Thanks."

"But there are other ways you could have resolved your conflict with Beth."

"I guess." I shrugged.

"And I never want to hear of you doing anything like this again. Ever."

"Okay."

"I'm serious, Tamar."

"*Okay.*"

"I worry about you."

"Me too," I said.

We sat in silence for a minute; then Dad turned the volume back up and we watched *Jeopardy!* and finished our drinks. I snuck looks at him while he was yelling out the answers to the hapless contestants who stared blankly at Alex Trebek. Dad's skin was as pale as glue, and his light brown hair was flat and dingy.

"Who is Mahatma Gandhi! Jesus, these people don't even deserve to be on *Jeopardy!*"

"Dad, when's the last time you went outside?"

"I don't know," he said.

"Do you want to go for a walk?"

"No."

I frowned.

"In case you haven't noticed, T, I'm a bit of a gimp right now." He gestured to his cast.

"You're getting around on your crutches all right."

He snorted.

"I want you to walk with me down the street to the mailbox and back."

He grumbled.

"Come on, it'll be good to get some fresh air."

I slung his arm around my shoulders, helped him to his feet and handed him his crutches. He waved me off and pulled his coat on over his robe. Then he gingerly slid into his boot, teetering ever so slightly.

The snow was lavender under the light of the moon. There were no cars or people around, and our street was quiet except for the occasional yelp of a dog.

My dad breathed deeply. "Feels like it's getting warmer out."

"It'll be spring pretty soon."

He shook his head as if he didn't believe it.

There was a huge stack of bills, late-payment notices and fliers in our mailbox. No one had picked up the mail for weeks.

On our way back home, I noticed rust-colored clouds creeping over the pockmarked face of the moon. "Look at that." I pointed.

We stood on the sidewalk and watched as the splotch of clouds spread across the moon like a bloodstain. The whole sky darkened to a reddish brown and the thin wisps of clouds turned coppery. I shivered, and my dad adjusted his crutches and put his arm around my shoulders.

And then my dad tipped his head back and howled. It was a low, mournful sound that seemed to come from somewhere deep and secret inside his body. Well, that settles it, I thought. My dad is officially insane. Then a dog across the street yowled, and another one from a backyard close by woofed and whined. Dad howled again, and more dogs joined in, then more dogs, from two, three, four streets away, and then I howled too, right up into that strange dark shadow. Again and again we howled at the blemished moon, until the entire neighborhood was a loud and crazy chorus of bawling, wailing, yelping cries and shrieks and moans.

Once the murky smudge had drifted across the face of the moon, we stopped howling and listened to the dog choir carry on, their lonesome sounds echoing off the houses, their owners pleading with them to be quiet. We laughed for a long time, holding our guts as if to keep them from spilling out onto the sidewalk. I couldn't remember the last time I had felt so good, so free.

We continued our slow walk home. When we got inside, I put the mail on the kitchen table, then helped Dad get set up on the couch again with his beer cans, ruler and pencil, and his X-Acto knife.

"Goodnight, Dad," I said on my way upstairs.

"Hey, Tamar?"

"Yeah?"

"Thanks for the walk." He smiled shyly at me, like a small boy.

That night I dreamt that I was naked and Don and Karen from Cruisy Chicken were spraying me with a hose, and all this curdled white stuff was coming out of the hose and sticking to me in nasty white globules. It got in my eyes and burned them and I couldn't see, and I was inhaling it, and I couldn't say anything because every time I opened my mouth, they would spray it in my mouth. It was horrible.

In the morning, the phone woke me up. I went into the parents' room and picked it up. It was Don.

"Tamar, we need you to come in for a staff meeting today."

Chicken fat, I thought. That's what the white stuff was. Sick.

"Tamar?"

"Yeah?"

"Ten o'clock. Today."

"Do I need to wear my uniform?"

"No, that won't be necessary," he said, and he hung up.

I barely had enough time to make it there and had to chase the bus for two blocks, waving my arms like an imbecile. When it finally stopped for me, I got on, breathless.

When I got to Cruisy Chicken, I was ushered into Don's office. Karen was sitting in the only other chair, so I had to stand. There were no other staff members there.

"Tamar, Karen and I don't feel that you can keep up the fast pace that we need to see from our employees."

I looked at Karen. She was eyeing my head suspiciously. I had worn a dark-blue bandana instead of my wig.

"We're letting you go."

"Oh." Something crumpled inside my chest.

"Your last check will be mailed to you."

"What about the uniform?" I asked, my voice trembling.

"That's yours to keep."

I sighed and walked out. *Don't cry don't cry don't cry don't cry.* I had been fired. Fired! From Crappy Chicken! I was too slow! I was too stupid! For Crappy Chicken! I was a total failure.

I walked to the bus stop with my head down, my face burning with shame. I blinked hard to keep my tears from gushing out. I had to wait twenty-eight minutes for the next bus.

"*Look on the bright side,*" I heard Abby say. "*At least you don't have to work there anymore!*"

"*Yeah, that place sucked!*" Alia said. "*And your boss was a scummy perv!*"

I nodded in agreement, gulping back a sob.

When I got home, I threw the stupid uniform and the stupid red visor and the stupid TRAINEE name tag in the metal trashcan in the garage. I had paid for it all, but I didn't ever want to see it again.

But somehow it wasn't enough to just throw it away. I dragged the garbage can outside and got the jerry can Dad kept for filling the lawn mower. I sloshed gasoline over the clothes, then lit a match and flicked it into the can. The clothes made a loud *whoosh* as they ignited, and a brilliant plume of fire shot up from the can. While I stood and watched the bright flames lick the sides of the shiny can, I couldn't decide how to feel. I was angry, upset and delighted, all at the same time.

I had been fired! From my first real job! I was pathetic. Totally pathetic. But watching my uniform burn was immensely satisfying. The heat rising from the can felt good on my face. I began to feel a strange calm seep into me. I thought about my sisters. How they would have approved of this controlled burn. How they would have whooped and hollered and probably slapped me high fives and yelled "Fuck the man!" as they danced around the burning ring of fire.

After a few minutes, a pile of black and gray ash was all that remained of my service to Cruisy Chicken. I got a bucket of water from the kitched and poured it into the garbage can, then dumped the whole mess down the storm drain. Straight to hell with it.

I walked inside. Dad was still sleeping. I went upstairs. But I walked past my room and stopped in front of the closed white doors of my sisters' rooms. I took a deep breath, turned the knob of Alia's door and stepped inside.

It smelled stale. Except for her missing electric guitar and amp, everything was exactly as she had left it. Her clothes and books and pencil crayons and CDs were strewn about the room. I looked into the faces of the musicians plastered on her wall: Green Day, Kurt Cobain, The Ramones, Patti Smith, Bob Marley, Johnny Cash. Her dresser was littered with bottles of nail polish, cheap jewelry, notes, photos, pens, markers, hairbrushes still snarled with strands of her auburn hair. Out of curiosity, I pushed *Play* on her dust-covered stereo.

It's something unpredictable, but in the end it's right.
I hope you had the time of your life.

I leaned in to look closely at the photographs stuck around her mirror. She had her tongue out in a few of them. She had a tongue ring; I never knew that. Abby was in a lot of them.

I was only in one. It was an old, old picture, taken when I was four or five. They would have been three or four. I was pulling a red wagon that we used to have, and the two of them were sitting in it, their arms around each other. We wore bathing suits, all of us smiling, squinting into the sun. I peeled the photo away from the mirror and examined the back. There was no date, nothing. As the song ended, I looked around the room once more. It was almost as if I expected her to burst through the door and tell me to stop messing around with her stuff. I pressed *Off* and the word *GOODBYE* scrolled across the stereo. I left Alia's room with the photo in my hand.

I stood in the hall and stared at Abby's door for a few seconds before I opened it. The door creaked on its hinges. Inside, it smelled like Love's Baby Soft. She had obviously just cleaned her room before she went out that night; everything was in its place. I laughed when I looked at her bed. She had set up her pillows under the covers so it looked like she was in bed in case the parents checked. Apparently she had planned on not coming home that night. And she never had. I felt a wave of nausea wash over me. I sat on the edge of her bed and waited for it to pass. Maybe it was the intensity of her hot-pink walls. I had never liked pink, hot or otherwise. I spotted her diary on her bedside table. I opened the cover. *PRIVATE! KEEP OUT!* was written in bubble letters on the first page. I looked around the room.

It was heavy with stillness. Should I? I realized I had been holding my breath. I flipped to a page.

Steven asked me out today and I said yes! He is so cute and has the prettiest blue-green eyes. Story eyes!!! Ahhhhhhhhhh! I think I'm in love!

I rolled my eyes and flipped to another page.

Alia and I went to Layne's house last night. Steven and Eric and Josh were there and we all got drunk off vodka-orange juice. It was super fun but today I feel like a butt scrape.

I flipped again.

Tamar is such a lame-o bitch. I don't know what her problem is. Why is she so mean to us?

I snapped the diary shut and placed it back on her nightstand. I went to her makeup table, sat down on the little white bench and looked in the mirror. I looked at her lipsticks and eye shadows and concealers, all lined up in a neat row. I selected a bronze lipstick and put it on. I smacked my lips together. Then I realized the last lips that lipstick had touched were Abby's, and she was dead now. I shivered and wiped it off with the back of my hand. I opened her jewelry box. A ballerina popped up when it opened, but it didn't play music anymore. I sifted through her necklaces, earrings, bracelets. I picked out a silver ring with an oval turquoise stone in the center. I slipped it on my middle finger. It fit. I glanced once more around the tidy pink room, then quietly closed the door and tiptoed back to my room. I put the photo up in the corner of my mirror. I flopped down on my bed and studied the pretty blue ring on my finger. I wondered where Abby had gotten it. And it struck me as being infinitely sad that I would never know.

twelve

With no school and no job and no play rehearsal, I didn't
have a lot going on. I took the C-train down to 17th Avenue
with the intention of seeing Dr. Lung for acupuncture again,
but when I got there his office was locked up, and old news-
papers covered the windows. I peeked through a patch of
glass that hadn't been covered in paper. His desk and chairs
and all the paintings and Buddhas were gone. There was a
bucket and mop in the corner of the room, a bloated garbage
bag and a crushed coffee cup. Nothing else. It was like he
had never even been there.

I wandered around downtown, feeling empty. Then I
tripped and almost fell over some baskets outside a vintage
clothing store. The baskets were full of scarves. They were
three for ten dollars, so I bought three. One was burnt

orange with lines of gold thread running through it. One was black with Chinese dragons embroidered on it. The third was made of silk, with a gorgeous sunset scene and silhouettes of trees on it. I felt a sharp pang in my heart when I read the label, which said *Handpainted on Stellar's Island, British Columbia.*

I couldn't understand why my mom hadn't called or written yet. It was as if she had totally forgotten that she had a family.

I tried to look after my dad. I forced him to go out for a walk every day. We ordered pizza and rented movies and ate chips and ice cream. We only watched comedies. I practiced my lines for the play and made him read the other parts.

"Do you know the band Pink Floyd?" He looked up from the script.

"Yeah, of course I do. Everyone knows Pink Floyd, Dad."

"Do you like them?"

"Obviously, they're only, like, the best band of all time."

"Go rent *The Wizard of Oz.*" He handed me five bucks.

"Nah, I've already seen it ten times."

"Not like this you haven't." He gave my ribs a little poke with his crutch.

"Ow!"

"Get going." He jabbed at me again, and I scrambled off the couch.

When I got back, he had dusted off his old record player and put on the Pink Floyd album *Dark Side of the Moon.*

He took the needle off. "Okay, put it in," he said. I put the DVD in and pressed *Play*. The old MGM lion came on and roared. "Wait for it, wait for it, and…NOW!" He set the needle down and the album began. He hopped up and down on his good leg. "Mute it! Mute it!"

"Dad, what the hell are you doing?"

"Shh, just watch." He pointed to the screen.

And so I did.

My dad heaved his broken leg up on a footstool, then sank back into the couch and laughed. "Isn't that the damndest thing?"

It was probably the most awesome thing I had ever seen. I don't know how Pink Floyd did it, but it had to have been planned. The album matched the movie exactly, and it told Dorothy's story in a whole new way. A modern way. My favorite part was when "The Great Gig in the Sky" came on as her house was sucked into the tornado. Friggin' beautiful. And then it got all political on "Us & Them," when it was the Munchkins versus Dorothy's crew. Supercool. Dorothy Gale was a misfit, a freak. Her friends were all insane too. She didn't belong in Kansas or Oz. But she had people who loved her, and she believed in herself. And really, what more does a person need? I'll never forget that Dark-Side version of the movie as long as I live.

On my first day back to school after my suspension ended, I decided not to wear my wig. What was the point? Also, I had been having nightmares that someone else would try to rip it off. I wore my dark jeans and a tight black sweater and tied the new black dragon scarf around my head. I drew on my eyebrows and glued on my eyelashes and put on some black eyeliner and walked to school, steeling myself against whatever insults were about to be hurled at me. I prepared myself to play the role of school laughingstock.

The snow had almost melted, and water dripped from the trees like liquid crystals. I turned my face to the sun and felt its warmth.

I was completely floored by the reactions I got at school. It was nothing like the ridicule, wisecracks and torment I had expected to face. Some popular people actually acknowledged me in the halls! They nodded or said, "Hey, Tamar." And the look in their eyes wasn't pity. It seemed to be respect. Some preppy grade-twelve girls told me they loved my scarf! They asked where I got it. I couldn't believe it.

"That's so terrible what Beth did to you," a tall blond said to me.

"She's always been a bitch," said her friend. "I've known her since preschool. Even back then she was nasty."

"Uh, thanks, I guess."

The girls kept walking. They were two of the most popular girls at Canyon Meadows High. And they had just taken my side over Beth's.

At lunchtime I went to chess club, and for the first time ever, I beat Roy. I beat him! He told me he let me win, but I know he was lying, because he would never do that.

"So, if I beat you, and you were ranked fifth-best youth chess player in Canada, then that must mean that I'm the fourth best!"

"Not really," he said.

"No?"

"No, that's faulty logic."

"Oh, please. What are you, a Vulcan?"

He got this really hurt look on his face and I felt bad, but then he held up his left hand and separated his middle finger and his ring finger. He looked very serious. We both busted a gut laughing. Some of the other chess players shot us dirty looks because we had interrupted their concentration. We tried to stifle our laughter, but every time we looked at each other we started giggling again, so eventually we got up and left. We went to the cafeteria and split a small order of fries.

"I like your thing," Roy said, poking around in the fry basket.

"My thing?"

"Your...head...thing." He waved his fingers around his head.

"Thanks. Hey, what the hell happened to your uncle?"

"My uncle?"

"Dr. Lung."

"Oh, he had to go to China."

"China. Really?"

"Yeah, his friend is really sick. So he went to be with her."

"So he just dropped everything and split town?"

Roy shrugged. "What are ya gonna do? You never know how much longer people are going to live."

"No." I shook my head. "You never do."

On Tuesday when I walked into the theater for rehearsal, the whole cast burst into applause. I don't know why—it's not like I'm a hero or anything. I just did what anyone would have in the same situation. Maybe they thought I had cancer or something, I don't know.

"Welcome back, Tamar," Ms. Jane said as she put her arm around my shoulders and gave them a squeeze.

"Thanks," I mumbled, and I went to join the cast circle on stage. We did some vocal warm-ups and some interpretative dancing to loosen up, then began rehearsing the scene where Dorothy is screwing around on the farm and falls in the pigpen.

Beth didn't say anything to me except her lines. I noticed she still had a small scrape on her face from where I had scratched her. And I couldn't help feeling a little bit pleased about that.

After rehearsal, Scott McKinnon came up to me while I was tying my shoe.

"Hey, Tamar."

"Hey, Scott."

"What are you doing after this?"

I shrugged. "No plans."

"Want to grab a coffee?"

"Um, sure. Why not?"

I had no idea why Scott wanted to hang out with me all of a sudden. Maybe because in the eyes of the other kids, he was a freak, and now, so was I. Maybe somehow that bonded us. He had a gentle voice and eyes the color of caramel candies. If he wasn't gay, maybe I would have had a crush on him, but he was, so it didn't matter.

I told him about getting fired from Cruisy Chicken, which I hadn't told anyone except my dad. I still felt ashamed for not being able to keep that crappy-ass job.

"I got fired this year too," he said.

"Really? Why?"

"I was working at the movie theater, taking tickets, and when Andrea and her friends would come—this is when we were together—I would let them in for free. It wasn't hurting anybody. The movies would show regardless of how many people were in the theater. Anyway, one day the manager asked to see their tickets and Andrea's friend told him I always let them in for free."

I groaned.

"And that was the end of that."

"That sucks."

He shrugged. "I got another job right away."

"Where?"

"Mik's Milk." He took a sip of coffee. "I could probably get you in there too, if you're looking for another job. Someone just quit."

"Yeah, I am, actually. I can only work weekends though."

"Me too. We'd be working together." He smiled.

"Cool."

"Okay, I'll talk to Pete."

"Wow, thanks. That would be great."

"Hey, can I ask you something?"

I nodded and wrapped my fingers around my mug, letting the heat seep through my hands.

"Were you, um, were you born bald?"

"No." I pressed my lips together and sighed. "This is a recent development."

"Oh." He nodded. "Do you know why it happened?"

"I guess it's some rare disease or post-traumatic stress disorder or a combination of the two. Something like that."

"That's rough."

"Yeah, it's been a difficult year, to say the least."

He nodded. "Is it painful?"

"In some ways…"

He looked into his mug, and his caramel eyes glazed over. "I know what you mean."

I took a sip of coffee.

He looked into my eyes then, as if he was searching them for something. "Do you think it will grow back?"

"I don't know. I hope so."

We finished our coffee and Scott walked me home. The sky was a bruised plum. A group of song sparrows flitted by us, and I felt my heart lift a little.

"That was nice," he said as we came to the end of my driveway. "We should do it again sometime."

"Yeah," I said. "Definitely."

A wide grin split his face, and my heart skipped inside my chest.

The next day I wore the painted scarf from Stellar's Island and got loads of compliments on it too. I hoped my mom would bring me back more scarves from the island—if she ever came back, that is.

I overheard someone refer to me as "freaky bald chick," but I let it roll off…water… duck's back…whatever.

At lunchtime I met Roy at his locker.

"Hey, Tamar. Do you want to go see *Rocky* tonight at the cheap theater?"

"Um, I don't know. I think I have to wash my hair."

We both laughed.

"Come on, it's my favorite movie of all time."

"*Rocky*? Really?"

He nodded.

"Well, in that case…"

"Sweet."

All day there were annoying announcements over the PA for the grade twelves to hurry up and get their prom tickets because tomorrow was the last day they would be on sale. There were prom posters everywhere I turned. I overheard girls gushing about what their dresses were like or what the dresses they wanted were like, and who they were going with or who they wanted to go with. It was enough to make you puke. Canyon Meadows High always had its prom earlier than the other schools in Calgary. A few had theirs in April, and the rest in May; we were the only ones in March. It was supposed to help avoid conflict or public drunkenness or whatever the hell school administrators were afraid would happen if thousands of kids around the city were celebrating at the same time.

I met Roy at the theater at six forty-five. He bought popcorn and I bought black licorice, and we sat in the sticky red bucket seats and waited for the movie to start.

"Are you going to prom?" I asked him, just to make conversation.

"I don't know, are you?"

"No, I can't. I'm in grade eleven."

"Oh yeah, I forgot."

"Grade elevens can only go as a grade twelve's date."

"Okay, shh, it's starting!"

I rolled my eyes in the dark.

thirteen

The next day when I was at my locker between second and third period, getting my biology textbook, Eric Gaines tapped me on the shoulder. Eric is a semipopular grade twelve. He's on the rugby team and writes the sports column in our school paper. He sometimes says hello to me in the halls, I think because he hung around with my sisters. Eric is taller than any of the teachers. He has thick, charcoal-colored hair and his skin always looks tanned. He's what my mom would call big-boned. Solid, not fat.

"How's it going, Tamar?" He leaned against the locker beside mine.

"Oh, hey, Eric. What's up?"

"I was wondering…do you, uh, do you want to go to prom with me?" His ink-black eyes darted from my face to my feet and back again. He smiled, displaying a mouth full of teeth as white and square as Chiclets.

There was what you could call a pregnant pause as I considered the implications of his question. He stared down at me, mouth slightly agape, eyes shimmering with what looked like hope. I heard the voices of my sisters yelling in the back of my head, "Yes. Yes! YES! Say yes, you moron!!!"

"Um, okay. Sure."

"Yeah?" His dark eyes gleamed like two polished stones.

"Yeah."

"That's great! I'll pick you up tomorrow night at eight, okay?"

"Okay."

"See ya!" Then he hurtled away.

I stuck my face into the cool darkness of my locker and waited for my crimson blush to subside. I grinned into the sleeve of my coat. I knew it was cheesy and totally over-rated, but I couldn't help being a teensy bit excited. I was going to prom!

I ran home after school and ransacked my mom's and my sisters' closets for a suitable dress to wear to the prom. I settled on a floor-length black dress of Mom's with a slit up the side. It had rhinestone spaghetti straps and tiny sparkles running through it. I tried it on in the parents' room in front of their full-length mirror. I looked slender, leggy and, as Mom would say, busty, if only a little. I found a rhinestone choker in her jewelry box that matched perfectly. The only thing left was to decide what to do with my hair—or lack of hair, as it were. I tried on the black dragon scarf, but it didn't seem formal enough for a prom. I could wear my wig, but I felt so fake and weird about it now. What if I just went with a naked head? Could I do that? Should I?

I tried it out. I looked at myself from every angle. It certainly was…striking…daring, even. I would be the only bald eagle at the prom. That was…unique. But could I really do it? Could I pull it off? *"Maybe with some bright red lipstick,"* I heard Abby say. *"And some black eyeliner,"* Alia added.

The phone shrilled and I grabbed it before it could ring again. "Hello?"

"Hi."

"Hey, Roy."

"Tamar?"

"Yeah?"

"Will you be my prom date?"

My heart hurled itself against my chest like a caged bird. "I'd love to—"

"Cool."

"But I can't."

"Oh."

"Someone else already asked me."

"I see."

I could hear the disappointment in his voice, and I felt like yelling into the phone, "WHY DIDN'T YOU ASK ME SOONER, YOU STUPID IDIOT?"

"Well, have a good time then."

"Thanks."

"Bye."

"Bye, Roy."

I listened as he hung up, and then I belly flopped on the parents' bed and screamed into a pillow.

On Friday I couldn't hear any of my teachers. Their mouths were moving, but all I heard was, "Okay class, blah blah blah. And blah blah blah you know your blah will be coming up soon. So blah blah blah..." Paper airplanes were zooming around in my stomach all day. In rehearsal I screwed up a couple of lines, and it threw everyone off. It was embarrassing. But Cole Benson didn't even know all his lines yet and still had to call out "LINE!" for prompts all the time, so I didn't feel that bad about it.

Ms. Jane let us go early. She said our energy was through the roof but so scattered that we were useless.

"FOCUS, PEOPLE! That's your homework. I want you to go home and think about focus. What it means to really"—she put her hands to her temples and squeezed her eyes shut, took a big breath in and let out a huge, long, noisy breath through her nostrils—"*focus.*"

We all left the theater, chattering and giddy. Outside, it was raining lions and tigers and bears (Oh my).

Scott McKinnon walked me home, and I was grateful because he shared his umbrella.

"So my manager should be giving you a call this weekend," Scott said.

"Wow, that's great. Thank you so much."

"No problem."

I sidestepped a puddle. Scott walked right through it.

"Would you want to go to prom with me tonight, Tamar? As friends, obviously."

My belly did a backflip and I tried to keep my face composed. *Damn, damn, double damn.* "I'd really like to Scott, but I've already said yes to someone else."

"Oh yeah, that figures."

"Thanks for asking me though."

"I just thought it could be fun, that's all. I haven't danced in a while."

I nodded.

"Do you like to dance?"

"I don't know. It's been a few years. I probably shouldn't do it in public."

He laughed. "Every Wednesday is salsa night at the Rose and Bull."

"Yeah?"

"You should come with me sometime."

I smiled. His hair looked good wet. "I'd like that," I said.

I had a vision of me in a ruffly red salsa dress with my naked head, and Scott with a rose clenched between his teeth. I had to suppress my laughter.

"Well, I guess I'll see you on Monday then."

"Thanks for sharing your umbrella."

"Anytime." He spun on his heel and sauntered away. I watched his black umbrella bobbing up and down all the way to the end of my street, until he turned the corner. I wondered if he would always be with guys now or if he would make exceptions.

I heated up one of Mom's lasagnas for dinner. No one could make a lasagna as good as my mom's. No one. I flipped the calendar page over. She had been gone two weeks. Neither Dad nor I had heard from her since she'd left. Not a postcard, not a collect call, nothing. I guess they didn't allow contact with the outside world at her assram. That would be the only logical explanation.

"Dad! Dinner's ready!"

We were going to eat at the kitchen table like a proper family. Because I didn't want lasagna all over my lap, because TV rots your brain and dulls your eyes, because...because it was prom night, damn it. Dad sat down in his usual chair and I set a glass of milk down beside his plate. His eyes were bleary, and his hands had little red slashes all over them from his can cutting. We began to eat without saying grace, which still seemed strange to me.

"Dad?"

"Hm?"

"Do you think Mom's coming back?"

He set down his fork, swallowed and wiped at the sides of his mouth with his napkin. "I have no reason to believe otherwise," he said.

I nodded and we finished the meal in silence.

"Do you?"

"Yeah," I said quietly. "I do."

He looked at the calendar on the wall. "Is it March already?"

"Yeah."

"Well, she'll be back soon then."

"What if they brainwashed her?"

He smiled. "I think it was a little late for that, don't you?"

We both had a small laugh.

"It's a special night tonight, Dad."

"Oh? Why is that?"

"I'm going to prom."

"Really?"

"Yep."

"Well, that's fantastic, T. Who's the lucky fella?"

"His name is Eric Gaines. He's on the rugby team and he writes for the school paper."

"Wonderful."

"But get this…"

He leaned in.

"I was also asked by two other guys."

"Of course you were. You're probably the prettiest girl in school."

I shook my head and rolled my eyes.

"I *know* you're the smartest."

"*Dad!*"

"So, how did you make your decision?"

"Well, Eric asked me first and I said yes, and then the other guys asked me later, so I couldn't go back on my word."

"They must have been devastated."

"I doubt it."

"Well, I guess the early bird catches the worm, as they say."

"Are you calling me a worm?"

"I meant worm as in caterpillar, and caterpillar as in butterfly. Beautiful, elegant, graceful butterfly."

"Nice save, Dad."

"Will Eric be driving?"

"No, we'll probably walk."

"But it's pissing rain out there!"

"Okay, we'll drive then."

"And how old is Eric?"

"Um, twenty?"

"And still in high school? He must be a real dummy. I don't want my daughter going out with some dummy."

"Arrrgh! Okay, he's eighteen, but you have to let me ride in his car to prom! It's only a few blocks away."

"I'll think about it." He crossed his arms over his chest.

"Whatever. I have to go get ready." I ran upstairs and showered and scrubbed my head with the loofah. Tonight would be my head's big debut, and I wanted it to be clean and shiny. I smoothed lotion over my scalp and face. I put on some black eyeliner and then carefully drew the two dark arches of my eyebrows. I glued on my eyelashes. I actually saved a lot of time not having to shave, wax, trim, tweeze, shampoo, condition, blow-dry or style. Being bald was probably going to save me thousands of hours a year. I slipped into Mom's black dress and fastened the glittery necklace, then looked at myself in the parents' full-length mirror. Something was missing.

Lipstick.

I went into Abby's room and found a tube of brilliant red lipstick called Bleeding Heart. I put it on.

"*Perfect*," I heard Abby say.

I smiled into the mirror. She was right: red lipstick really pulled it all together. I tucked the lipstick into my purse in case I needed a touch-up during the night. It didn't creep me out this time that Abby had been the last person to wear it. It was kind of special, in a way, kind of nice.

I stood in front of the mirror again. The naked head was a shock even to me, but I couldn't wait to see the looks on everyone's faces when I waltzed in with it exposed. It was going to make for a memorable evening, that's for sure.

I went downstairs to sit with Dad while I waited for Eric to arrive.

He reached for his crutches and stood up when I came into the room. "Tamar! You look...stunning."

"Thanks, Dad."

"So, you're not wearing your..."

"Nope."

"Wow."

"Well, you know what they say: hair today, gone tomorrow."

He smiled. "That's a bold move, T."

"Don't you mean a *bald* move?"

"You're, like, the bald and the beautiful!"

"I could have my own show!"

"To baldly go where no one has gone before!"

"Yeah!"

"Fortune favors the bald!"

"That's right!"

"Bald as love!"

"B-A-L-D! Tell me what you'll give to me!"

"B-A-L-D! Super beauty you can see!"

"Bald and courageous!" I threw up my arms and we both collapsed onto the couch in a fit of laughter.

Eight o'clock came, and I caught myself tapping my foot and looking at the front door every two seconds.

Then it was eight ten.

Eight fifteen.

Eight twenty.

I could feel my dad staring at me during a commercial break.

"He probably just wants to be fashionably late," I said.

Dad nodded and turned back to the TV.

I went to the bathroom. I figured by the time I came out, Eric would be there, standing on the front doormat, introducing himself to my dad, apologizing for being late. Maybe he would even have a corsage for me. I put on my best smile to greet him and went out.

He wasn't there.

At eight thirty my dad said, "Do you have his phone number?"

"No."

"Maybe you should call directory assistance."

"He's probably just running late, Dad. Relax."

He shrugged and turned back to *Xena: Warrior Princess*.

I went to the kitchen and drank a glass of water. Then I had another one. Then I made some tea. It was eight forty-five.

"You had better call him, T. Something could have happened. He could have crashed his car on his way over here."

I rolled my eyes. "If he's not here by nine, I'll call."

"Up to you."

I went to check the answering machine to see if there was a message from Eric. There was a flashing red light on the display. I held my breath and pressed *Play*. The person had hung up without saying anything. I dialed *-6-9 to find out who had called. I didn't recognize the number but called it anyway. There was no answer. I let it ring about a thousand times. Then I hung up and dialed 4-1-1. The operator gave me three numbers for Gaines. None of the numbers matched the one *69 had given me. I tried the first one, but there was no one there named Eric. I tried the second one and there was no answer. I tried the third one and it was busy. I didn't know what to do. I went back into the living room and sat on the couch and watched the clock on the wall while my dad tried to find a good movie on TV. After five minutes I went back to the phone and tried the third number again. Still busy. I tried the second number. I let it ring a thousand times. It was nine twenty-eight. I went back to the living room and slumped against the couch.

"I'm sorry, sweetie," Dad said. "But I'm glad *I* get to hang out with you."

I closed my eyes. That didn't make me feel any better. It made me feel worse. I had been stood up. Stood up! And I could have gone with Roy or Scott, but no, I had to say yes to Eric "Bubblehead" Gaines and wait around all night for him to show, and now it was too late. I couldn't go with Roy or Scott, and Eric wasn't coming. I wasn't going to the prom. I could do nothing but sit on the couch in absolute misery with my sallow father and watch a kooky movie about boys who get leeches stuck to their dicks and then find a dead body in the woods.

I had been duped! He had done it to make me look stupid. To make me feel shitty. So he and his rugby friends could have a laugh at my expense. I was a pathetic loser who people pulled mean tricks on. Either that or he was killed in a terrible car crash on his way over here. Which is the only excuse he would have for not calling and not showing up, and the only way I could possibly save face in this whole sordid situation. I was, to say the least, crushed. I felt like one of the beer cans that guys like Eric Gaines put on the pavement and then stomp into a flat disk. I should have known that someone like him would never actually want to go to prom with someone like me.

"His loss," my dad said.

Yeah, right. I brushed away a tear that had escaped without warning.

"All right. I'm going to show you something," Dad said. "It's time." He reached for his crutches and got to his feet with some effort. I stayed seated, hanging my head in disgrace.

"Come on." He reached over and gave me a few light slaps on the arm. "No use feeling sorry for yourself."

I closed my eyes. Another hot tear slipped out.

"Let's go."

I pulled myself off the couch as if I weighed a thousand pounds and followed my dad through the laundry room and into the garage. He flicked on the light.

Two little airplanes and a helicopter hung from the ceiling; they were made entirely out of beer cans. Their shiny aluminum bodies glimmered in the brightness of the bare lightbulb. The top shelf held four beer-can model cars. Dad reached to pick up the one closest to him.

"I thought I'd start with what I know, so I made a Honda." He glanced at me, a boyish grin curling his mouth.

"This here is a replica of the first car Honda ever made. The S500. It debuted in 1962." He handed me the car. "It had a five hundred thirty-one cc engine with forty-four horsepower at eighty-five hundred rpms, weighing in at fifteen hundred pounds. This one weighs about two."

"A sports car." I opened and closed one of its tiny doors. "Cool."

"But then I thought, why should I just stick to Honda?" He grabbed the next can-car on the shelf and handed it to me.

"A Lambo?"

"Yep! And check this out." He slid the car door up to open it.

"Just like the real ones!"

"Yeah! You know, I've always said I wanted a Lamborghini. Now I actually have one." He laughed and so did I. "Then I made this." He pointed to the next vehicle on the shelf, a Hummer. "Just for fun, you know."

I smiled. I couldn't picture my dad driving around in a Hummer. He was more of a wood-paneled-station wagon type of guy.

"And this one I just finished today." He gingerly picked up a Model-T Ford.

I put the other cars back on the shelf so I could hold it. I turned it over in my hands, examining all the tiny details and miniature pieces.

"Kind of gives a whole new meaning to the name Tin Lizzie, doesn't it?"

"Tin Lizzie!" Dad laughed. "I never thought of that. That's perfect!"

"These are really good, Dad."

"Nah."

"Yes!" It was true. I was amazed at what he had made in the weeks since he'd broken his leg. "You could sell them." I handed the Tin Lizzie back to him.

"You think so?"

"Sure, why not?"

"I don't know. It's just junk, really."

"No way. They're awesome." I touched the propeller of the helicopter. Its blades spun multicolored beer logos around and around, until they all blurred together.

"Well, I'm glad you like them."

"I do."

"You can have one, if you want."

"Really?"

"Sure, any one you like. Or I could make another one, just for you."

"Cool." I let my eyes slide over the cars and aircraft. I kept coming back to the Model-T. It was so classic. I picked it up off the shelf. "Can I have this one?"

"It's yours."

"Wow, thanks, Dad."

He put his arm around me and gave me a sideways hug. I let myself be squished into his rib cage and caught his crutch before it toppled over.

fourteen

That weekend I started working at Mik's Milk and Gas.
I had to wear a uniform, but at least I didn't have to pay
for it. It was a blue-and-white-striped shirt with that stupid
thumbs-up cat on the breast pocket, blue polyester pants
and a baseball cap that also had the cat on it. I had to learn
how to work the till, check lotto tickets, make coffee, pump
gas and diesel, check oil, wash windshields, fill fluids and
pump propane. I hated pumping propane because it smelled
disgusting, like being trapped inside a crate full of rotten
eggs. I was terrified that a tank would explode on me.
If Scott was around, I would get him to do the propane,
but he was usually out pumping gas and yakking with
truckers. Scott trained me and it was only the two of us
working, so that was good.

"This is your emergency button. Wear it around your neck at all times." He handed me what looked like a green plastic doorbell on a chain.

"What does this do?"

"If you press it, the security company will call the store. If you don't answer, they'll wait five minutes and call again. If you don't answer the second time, they'll recommend that the police send someone by to check on you."

"I could be dead by then."

"Exactly."

And that's pretty much how things worked at Mik's. I still made five forty an hour, even though I was risking my life every time I filled a propane tank or pumped gas for someone who refused to put out a cigarette. Once in a blue moon I made a dollar or two in tips, but it was usually from some scuzzwart in a pimped-out Honda or a little shiny truck with a lift kit, desperate for a date. A lot of kids from school came in and sucked up to me to try to get me to sell them smokes.

"Hi, Tamar. I really like your, uh, hat."

"Tamar! You look so great today! I just love your new look. You're so gutsy." Etcetera, etcetera. Sometimes I'd sell them the ciggies, sometimes I wouldn't. It depended on my mood that day and if I thought they deserved to die of lung cancer or not.

Mik's Milk was okay. Instead of smelling like a grease trap, I smelled like gasoline, diesel and propane. Delightful.

Roy had ended up going to prom with Marcy Mavis, aka Glinda, the Good Witch of the North. I could just see her on Roy's arm, wearing a pink ball gown, lighting up the room with her sunshine-yellow hair. I tried not to picture Marcy and Roy kissing in the limo, at the hotel after-party, in the indigo light of dawn, but I knew they probably had. And that knowledge sat heavy in the pit of my stomach, like rotten fruit. I guessed I should just be glad that he hadn't gone with Beth. She had asked him, of course. But he'd said no. Obviously. After what she'd done to me, his friend, he was morally obligated to say no. Big Boobs Dewitt sure didn't play her cards right on that one. Scott went with Andrea, for old times' sake, I guess. I heard he wore a pink tuxedo. He was really coming all the way out of the proverbial closet.

I didn't see Eric Gaines at school for a while, and I secretly hoped he had died. Okay, okay, I didn't really hope he was dead, but I hoped he was seriously injured. Then one day, not long after the heart-crushing prom stand-up, I saw him hunched over a water fountain. My heart plummeted into my belly, then bounced back up to my throat. Should I confront him? Or should I avoid him?

I had to know, so while he noisily slurped up water, I went and stood behind him, preparing to call him a shitfaced asshole. When he turned around and saw me, he looked right through me as if I were invisible and started to walk away. I moved to block his path.

"Hey, Eric. What the hell happened to you on prom night?"

"Oh." He shrugged. "I changed my mind."

"*Pff, what an assmunch*," I heard Alia say in the back of my head.

"You could have called me. I thought maybe something terrible had happened to you."

He shrugged again, as if it was no big deal, as if he hadn't done anything wrong, as if he hadn't left me totally and utterly devastated.

I rolled my eyes and speed-walked away, holding my head up high. I vowed never to speak to him again as long as we both shall live. Jerkass.

I caught up with Roy at his locker.

"Guess what I got this weekend?" he said, grinning.

"Uh, venereal disease?"

"No…" He frowned at me.

"Oh. What?"

"I got my full license."

"Really? That's great. Congratulations."

"Thanks. Want to go for a drive sometime?"

"Um…yeah, sure."

"How about today after school?"

"Okay, I guess that could work." My dad would assume I was at rehearsal, so I wouldn't bother asking his permission. He would never let me drive with Roy because he was only eighteen.

"Cool, I'll meet you here at last bell."

"Great." The valves in my heart fluttered as he sauntered away.

We got Coke slushies and then climbed into Roy's mom's red Toyota Tercel and cruised south. I switched the radio to CJSW, the University of Calgary's student-run indie station. It was playing "Walk on the Wild Side," and we sang along with Lou Reed:

Went to the Apollo, you should have seen him go, go, go.
They said, "Hey, Sugar, take a walk on the wild side."
I said, "Hey, babe, take a walk on the wild side."
All right. Huh!

We laughed, and I stuck my hand out the window, letting the warm spring air rush past my fingertips.

Roy never went over the speed limit. His driving was smooth and calculated. He seemed pretty comfortable at the wheel, as if he had been driving his entire life instead of only a year. I knew he was nothing like the boys who had played Chicken with my sisters in the backseat. He drove us out to The Big Rock in Okotoks.

The Big Rock is a massive chunk of mountain that hitched a ride with a glacier sixteen thousand years ago. In its original form it weighed nearly seventeen thousand tonnes.

According to Blackfoot legend, it split down the middle when bats attacked it to make it stop rolling.

Roy and I scaled the larger piece of rock and sat down when we made it to the summit. We looked out over the pale yellow fields that lay in all directions. The sky above us was flaming orange and pink and gold.

"I have some other news." Roy scratched a piece of shale into the rusted rock face beneath us.

"What's that?"

"I've been accepted to the engineering program at UBC."

"Really?"

He nodded.

"Roy! Congratulations!"

"Thanks."

"That's great!"

"Yeah."

"So, are you going to go?" I tried to swallow the stone that had lodged itself in my throat.

"Well, yeah. UBC was my first choice."

I looked down. "That's so great."

"You could come with me, Tamar. We could rent an apartment together. We could eat sushi, we could go to Science World—that big silver dome, you know?"

"That would be amazing," I said. "But I have to finish high school."

"There are millions of high schools in Vancouver!"

"Millions?"

"Okay, hundreds."

I flicked a mosquito off my arm.

"Promise me you'll at least think about it. I would love to have you there," he said, staring into my eyes.

"Okay." I tried to smile. "I'll think about it."

"You're my best friend."

"And you're mine."

Roy put his arm around me then, and I leaned into him, resting my head on his shoulder. He tilted my face toward his and ever so gently kissed my lips. It was sublime and pure and perfect. I wished it could go on forever.

He pulled away first, smiling, his eyes glazed. I tucked my head back into the warm crook between his neck and shoulder. Coyotes yipped and whined in the distance as Roy and I watched the scarlet sunset melt into a searing pinprick of light, then disappear.

I felt a great chasm divide what could have been my heart, splitting it right down the middle and crumbling it to pieces.

fifteen

In biology class we learned that the average person takes seven minutes to fall asleep. That night it took me about seven hours. My mind spun with thoughts of Vancouver. And beautiful British Columbia. I could imagine myself living beside the ocean, going to sleep to the sound of gently lapping waves. Imagine the mountains right there at my doorstep, and the cherry blossoms floating through the streets. No one could ever tell me what I could and couldn't do or say or think or wear because the parents would be an entire province away. No one would know about my sisters or my hair or my life history as a geeky, awkward, loser chick. I could start fresh. Get a clean slate. It was an incredibly exciting possibility.

In the week that followed, I was entirely consumed by thoughts of Vancouver. I checked out books about it from the library, I read about it on the Internet, I asked Scott about it, because he had grown up there. I told the guidance counselor, Ms. Nixon, that my family might be moving to Vancouver, and she found a high school right near the university that I could transfer to, no problem.

I imagined myself going to coffeehouses in Vancouver where artists and writers and actors hung out, where people would admire my smooth and shapely head and my courage, and we would have interesting conversations about music and literature and film and art and theater, and maybe, just maybe, I would feel like I belonged.

Roy and I went garage sale-ing on the weekend. He said he wanted to start collecting kitchen stuff so he would be all ready to set up his apartment in Vancouver.

"Do you like these?" he asked, holding up an ugly set of mustard-colored bowls.

"It doesn't matter if I like them or not."

"It might," he said.

At a garage sale in Woodbine, I found an old Nintendo with two controllers and a Duck Hunt gun. But the only game that came with it was Tetris. I bought it anyway and hooked it up that night for Dad and me to play. Dad loved it. We got supercompetitive and ended up playing until two in the morning for the first couple of nights we had it. I have never heard my dad swear so much as he did when we were playing Tetris. He got better, though, with practice. We both did.

"You know, T, Tetris is a lot like life."

"How do you figure?"

"Well, you never know what's going to come next, but you sure as shit have to deal with whatever it is."

Finally, the second of April arrived, the day my mom was due back. The night before, I had cleaned the whole house until it sparkled and made peanut-butter-chocolate-chip cookies, her favorite. I got fifty bucks from Dad and bought a bunch of groceries, stuff I knew she liked: salad fixings, rice cakes, fruit, yogurt—what Dad called rabbit food.

I could barely sit still all day in my classes because I couldn't wait to get home and hug her and tell her I had missed her and that I loved her. After school, I burst through the front door ready to squeal, but she wasn't there. And neither was Dad. I checked the answering machine. No new messages. I stood in the kitchen and looked out the sliding-glass door into our backyard. Two young deer were devouring the new purple crocuses. Their eyes were like puddles of liquid chocolate. I tapped on the glass and they skittered away.

I heard the front door open and my heart leapt. "MOM!" I raced to the door.

"Nice to see you too, T," said Dad. He clasped a bottle of wine in one hand and a bouquet of flowers in the other, using his crutches like a pro.

"What's that for?"

"To celebrate your mom's return, of course." He went into the kitchen and put the wine in the fridge and the flowers in a vase. Then he washed his hands and started chopping up vegetables.

"Dad, what are you doing?"

"What's it look like?"

"I—"

"I'm making my world-famous spaghetti sauce."

"Dad!"

"What?"

"You're back!" I threw my arms around him and didn't let go. He peeled me off and told me to start chopping garlic.

The sauce smelled so good, I nearly cried. I sat at the kitchen table and did my homework. Then I filled out a questionnaire Ms. Jane had given us to help us really get to know our characters and presumably play them with more authority. It was full of silly questions:

Auntie Em

What is your favorite color?

Sunshine yellow.

What is your astrological sign?

Cancer—I can get crabby.

If you were stranded on a desert island and could only bring one other character in The Wizard of Oz, *whom would you bring and why?*

Tin Man, because I could make a boat out of him and row away. Plus, he's a sweetheart.

Dad and I waited as long as we could. At nine thirty he put the pasta on to boil, because we were both starving.

"We'll save her some," he said.

"Yeah," I whispered.

We ate in silence and sat at the table afterward, staring at the clock. We moved into the living room and watched *The Late Show*. Then *The Late Late Show*. Then the news. Still no Mom.

"I knew it," I said.

"What?"

"She's not coming home."

The look on his face was so dejected, so destroyed, that I wished I had kept my mouth shut. But it was too late; I couldn't take my words back. I suppressed a yawn.

"I'm tired. I'm going to bed."

"Okay."

"Goodnight, Dad."

"Goodnight, T." He reached toward me and I gave him an awkward, sitting-down hug. I pressed my face into his shoulder for a second but refused to break down in front of him.

I ran up to my room and collapsed into bed. Tears flooded my pillow. My own mother had run away from home. The knowledge pierced my heart with a slow and terrible pain.

sixteen

I woke up to the sound of the phone ringing. Warm, white sunlight flooded my room. I sat up in bed and strained to hear what Dad was saying. All I could make out was the low rumble of his voice, but something about it made me feel anxious.

After a few minutes there was a knock at my door.

"Yeah?"

Dad pushed the door open and stood on one leg in the doorway, supported by his crutches. "Your mother is in the hospital."

"What?"

"There was an accident at the farm. One of the cows kicked her in the head."

I laughed. "Really?"

"She has a very serious concussion, Tamar. She couldn't even remember her last name until this morning."

"Holy cow."

"Not funny."

"Sorry."

"We have to go to Stellar's Island General Hospital and pick her up."

"Okay. Let's go."

"I can't drive." He gestured to his broken leg.

"Oh yeah. Neither can I."

"I know."

"So…how are we going to pick her up?"

"You tell me."

"What about Roy?" I said. My heart leaped into my throat.

"Your boyfriend?"

"Dad, I don't have—"

"That Chinese kid."

"He's half Chinese, half white."

"Does he have his license?"

"Yeah, of course, but…"

"But what?"

"I don't know. It's just that it's so far and…"

"Tamar."

"Yeah?"

"That's what friends are for."

I nodded and swallowed. "Okay."

"You ask him first and then I'll talk it over with his parents."

I pulled on jeans and a T-shirt and went to the kitchen to call Roy. He answered, sounding sleepy. It was eight thirty in the morning. We were on the road by ten o'clock

I propped Dad up in the back of the Tercel with blankets and pillows, his legs stretched across the backseat. He got carsick if he wasn't the one driving, so he took a couple of Gravols before we left and was sound asleep by the time we merged onto Sarcee Trail.

"Thank you so much for helping us out, Roy," I said. "This is—"

"It's no problem." Roy flicked his turn signal and changed lanes to pass a semi. "It'll be fun." He smiled.

"You're the best."

His hand left the steering wheel and closed over mine.

When we stopped in Banff for gas, I got a bag of licorice allsorts, just like old times. I knew Dad would appreciate them when he woke up. Roy and I drank strong coffee and cranked up the classic rock station. We sang along with The Doors, Neil Young, Pink Floyd and Creedence Clearwater Revival all the way through the Rockies.

"Sometimes I feel like I was born in the wrong decade." I sighed, gazing out the window at the massive, cloud-capped mountain peaks.

"What do you mean?"

"Most of the time I feel like I don't belong here. I don't understand pop culture, fashion trends, current music, nothing."

"Well, today's music sucks, so you're not missing much."
I laughed. "Yeah?"

"Seriously, our generation is experiencing a devastating drought in quality music. The music of today is not art. It's advertising. Its purpose is to sell us crap we don't need."

"Look at that!" I pointed to a steep blue mountain cliff where a bighorn sheep teetered precariously, nibbling at a tuft of grass. "It's going to fall!"

"No, I don't think so," said Roy. "They're experts at that sort of thing." Then he braked hard, and my collarbone strained against the seatbelt. A mama black bear and her cub lumbered across the highway. The mom was huge, but I could have picked the cub up and cuddled him in my arms. The man in the car behind us got out and started snapping photos. The adult bear stood up on her hind legs, raised her snout in the air and began to move toward our car.

"Yikes." I rolled up my window.

Roy honked the horn, once, twice, three times. The bear was still approaching. She ambled right up to my side of the car, her beady black eyes boring into mine. She pressed her huge nose against the glass.

"Roy..."

Then Roy laid on the horn for a good ten or fifteen seconds, and the bear dropped back down to all fours and led her cub safely across the road.

Dad chuckled from the backseat. "That was a close one."

My heart was pounding as we pulled away, but the tourist behind us was still taking pictures, oblivious to any danger.

We were all quiet until we passed the intense aquamarine of Lac des Arcs.

"It's hard to believe colors like that even exist," I said.

"Everything exists," said Roy.

"I don't know about that," I said.

"Yep."

"What about a three-horned unicorn?"

"Well, it exists in your imagination, doesn't it?"

"I guess so."

"Then it exists."

"What about a parallel universe?"

"For sure."

"You really think so?"

"Oh yeah."

I checked the backseat to see what Dad thought of all this, but he had dozed off again. "Will you be taking a philosophy class at UBC?"

"Yeah, I want to. If I have room for an elective."

"Then you'll have to tell me what they say about your theory of total existence."

"I will," he said, nodding. "I definitely will."

"Maybe there's an alternate me living in a parallel universe right now with all of my hair."

"Maybe."

I reached under my dragon scarf and touched my bare scalp. A pang of sadness shot through me. I missed running my fingers through my hair. Smoothing down flyaways. Twisting strands around my finger while I daydreamed. I missed my hair. I really did.

"What do you think you would be doing right now if you had hair? How would your life be any different?" Roy said.

I looked over at him. His outline wavered as my vision became blurry. "You have no idea what this is like for me, Roy. So just don't even—"

"Look, all I'm saying is that you're still you. You're still Tamar Robinson. There's nothing you could have done before that you can't do now."

"Easy for you to say."

"Okay, what could you have done with hair that you can't do now?"

"I could have been..."

"What?"

"I could have been popular, okay? I could have been someone that people thought was...was...pretty. Someone worth knowing. Now I'm just a hairless freak show."

"Tamar, listen to me. It's not up to other people. It's up to you. You get to decide how you feel about being bald, and then other people will act accordingly. If you want to sulk around about it, then yeah, maybe people will feel sorry for you or whatever, but you also have the chance to really wear it well, to really *work it, girl!*" He snapped his fingers and waggled his head.

I giggled.

"It's sort of like the glass."

"What glass?"

"That glass that can be half empty or half full."

"I don't see how it's anything like that glass."

"Well, think about it this way. Have you lost a part of yourself—"

"Yes, yes I have."

"*Or,* have you gained an opportunity to redefine yourself—you know, revamp your image?"

"Have you been watching *Oprah* with your mom again?"

"So?"

"Jeez, Roy." I rolled my eyes.

"Well, it's up to you."

"Yeah, it is."

"Go ahead and wallow in your own swamp of self-pity."

"I—"

"*Or* you can simply accept it for what it is and let the real you,"—he poked me on the shoulder—"the *real* beautiful you deep inside shine out."

I turned away from Roy to stare out the window, letting his words sink into me. The sun burst out from behind the clouds and blinded us for a second. Roy put his visor down and so did I.

We didn't speak again until we were in British Columbia. Dad had to pee, so we pulled in to a truck stop in a town called Golden. We sat down in a sticky green booth and ordered club sandwiches, French fries and Cokes. The bleached-blond waitress scratched her head with her pen. It seemed like she had lived a hundred lives before this one, all of them less than satisfactory. I watched through the grease-smeared window as the truckers pulled in and out. I wondered what it would be like to drive back and forth across the country, not calling anywhere your home.

By the time we hit Revelstoke, I had decided I liked BC better than Alberta. It was so green, so luscious, so beautiful. As we drove over the bridge, the river below glittered sapphire, and I longed to jump over the concrete rail into its clear, clean coldness, even though I knew it would freeze every cell in my body.

My dad was wide awake now and thought it would be a good idea to play car trivia, something my sisters and I used to despise on family road trips.

"Who was Canada's first female prime minister?"

"Kim Campbell," Roy said. "Too easy."

"Okay, Tamar. What is the capital of Nunavut?"

"Um, it starts with an *I*."

"That is an insufficient answer."

"Iqaluit," Roy said.

"Very good, Roy. Next question is for Tamar. Tamar, what is Laura Secord famous for?"

"Chocolate."

"Try again."

"Ice cream."

"Think historically."

I rolled my eyes. I hated car trivia.

"Laura Secord was a spy," Roy said.

"Getting warmer."

"She warned the British of the Americans' plan to attack Canada in the War of 1812, and because of her the British won the war," Roy said.

"That's right! Okay, when did Alberta officially become a Canadian province?"

"1900," Roy said.

"Nope."

"Who cares?" I said.

"Tamar, I thought you liked car trivia."

"No, actually I don't. I hate car trivia. I've never liked it and I never want to play it again as long as I live."

"Oh," my dad said, deflated. "I didn't realize you felt that way."

"I kind of like it," Roy mumbled.

I shot him a mean look.

Roy focused on the road, his dark eyebrows knit together in concentration. My dad adjusted the pillow behind him and gazed out the back window, his blue-gray eyes clouded over with…something—suffering, maybe.

I rolled down the window, letting a blast of cold air rush through and flush out the stale air in the car.

"Do you have any water up there?"

I tossed a water bottle into the backseat. I watched in the rearview mirror as Dad popped another Gravol and washed it down with a swig of water, then leaned his head against the car door and closed his eyes.

We passed mountains and trees and birds and cars and trucks and restaurants and gas stations and motels and casinos and more trees and more trees and more trees. I let the kilometers wash over me, the *rush-rush* sound of the road filling my head. I missed my sisters. I missed my mother. I missed my life the way it used to be, when I still had hair and my whole family was alive and well.

The evening sky was a magenta banner over Shuswap Lake as we drove past a place called Blind Bay. The rolling hills were golden pink, and the setting sun reflecting off the water turned the lake into liquid fire. Dad was asleep again and Roy was scanning the radio stations. The only one coming in clearly had a preacher going on about an afterlife of eternal damnation. I snapped it off.

"So..." Roy said.

"So?"

"You hungry?"

"Nope."

"Thirsty?"

"No."

"I need to stop for gas pretty soon."

"Okay."

"We'll stop in Kamloops."

"Fine."

"What do you think they call people from Kamloops?"

"I don't know. Kamloopians?"

"What do you think they call people from Kamloops who work in orchards?"

"No idea."

"Fruit loops!" He laughed and slapped the steering wheel with glee.

"Did you just make that up?"

"Yeah!"

I snickered. "You're such a geek."

"I know, but it suits me, don't you think?"

"Yeah, I do." I reached over and rubbed my hand over his soft black hair. I let it linger at his hairline and gave his neck a few gentle squeezes. Then I folded my hands in my lap.

A pale crescent moon popped out between the low mountains. My dad snored quietly in the backseat, his mouth hanging slightly open. I pushed my seat back and let my eyes rest for a few minutes.

When I opened them again, the car was stopped and Roy was gone. A fierce panic rose up in me, but I forced it down. As my eyes adjusted to the dark, I saw that we were parked at a gas station. Dad was sleeping soundly, so I let him be and went inside, locking the car doors behind me. A grizzled man with a gray beard stood behind the till, and he eyed me up and down as I entered. I shivered and wrapped my arms around myself. Kamloops was cold.

"Good evening, Miss," he said in a cigarette-stained voice.

"Hi."

I didn't see Roy anywhere, and the wave of panic threatened to surge again. I walked to the cooler to pick out a drink. There was no one else in the store, and I could feel Graybeard's eyes on me. I grabbed a chocolate milk and went to the counter.

"From Alberta, eh?" he said.

"Um, yeah, is it that obvious?" I looked down at my clothes.

"Nah, your plates, sweetie." He nodded toward the Tercel.

"Oh, right."

He scanned the chocolate milk and squinted out the window. "Wild rose country, eh?"

"That's what they say." I shrugged.

"Knew a wild Rose once myself, hehe." He smiled widely, displaying black holes where his canine teeth should have been.

"Ha."

Roy walked out of the men's room then, and I was so relieved my knees felt weak. He took a Coke from the cooler and came up to the counter, setting it down beside the milk. "And the gas," he said.

"This your boyfriend?"

"No."

"Yes," Roy said, sliding his arm around my waist like it belonged there.

And then a funny thing happened that I can't describe exactly, except to say it was sort of like an egg inside me cracked open, but instead of a little yellow yolk inside, it was a big gushy-girly-giddy-happy-go-lucky-warm-fuzzy yolk. And I stood up a little straighter and probably wore a dopey grin as I paid Graybeard.

"Lucky guy." He winked at Roy as we left the store.

We got onto the Coquihalla Highway, and I kept stealing little looks at Roy when headlights illuminated his face. He wore an expression of contentment, the right side of his mouth turned up a little higher than the left when he looked over at me.

"What are you thinking about?" he asked.

"Nothing." I turned and stared straight ahead, a grin stretching my lips despite my attempts to keep a straight face.

"Are you okay?"

"For the most part, yeah."

"Good."

I found a radio station that wasn't too fuzzy. It was mostly crappy soft rock, but at least it was something. I could just make out the black shapes of mountains silhouetted against the night sky, and I wished I could see the scenery instead of neon signs.

"If you could have any superpower, what would you want to have?" I asked Roy.

"Hm, that's a tough one."

I nodded.

"I think I would want the ability to read people's minds."

"Really? Why?"

"So I would know what other people were thinking about, and I could predict their next moves."

"I would never want to be able to read everyone's thoughts. I think it would be scary."

"It probably would be, but it would be useful too."

"Give me one example of how it would be so useful."

"Well, like, say I was driving down the highway at night, in the middle of butt-nowhere, BC, and there was some dude approaching me in the oncoming lane."

Cars zoomed past us at lightning speeds. I shifted in my seat. My left foot was asleep and my back hurt from sitting all day. "Yeah?"

"I could see his thoughts, right? So I would know that he wasn't watching the road or paying attention to driving at all. I'd know if he was drifting off to sleep or thinking about cheating on his wife or whatever, so I could pull off to the shoulder until he passed instead of being in imminent danger by being on the road with him."

"So wouldn't it be a better use of your superpower choice to be able to instantly regrow your organs and skin in case you got hurt?"

"Maybe, but what about the other people in the car with me?" He turned to look at me, then adjusted the rearview mirror to check on my sleeping father.

"Well, I guess they'd be screwed."

"Pretty much. What power would you want?" he asked.

"I think I would want the ability to see into the future," I said.

"Don't you think that would get boring though? You would never have any surprises."

"Yeah, but I would always be prepared for what was coming next."

Suddenly my dad stuck his face up front and sucked at his teeth. "Are we there yet?"

Roy jumped a little, then laughed. "No, not quite yet, Mr. Robinson."

Dad stared at Roy in the rearview mirror for a long moment. "Call me David."

I turned around. "We just went through Merritt."

"Well, I can feel my back teeth floating, so you had better pull over, toot sweet."

Roy laughed and pulled over at the next rest stop. All of us got out. I felt pins and needles in my legs, and I did some jumping jacks to get the blood pumping back to them.

When we were back in the car, Roy tried and failed to cover up a big yawn.

"How are you doing up there, Roy?" Dad asked.

"Well, to tell you the truth, Mr. Robinson...uh...David, I'm getting kind of tired."

"Yeah?"

"I've never driven this far before, and, well, you know..."

"Sure, sure. I understand. No problem, we'll get a hotel in the next town. It will be cheaper than spending the night in Vancouver anyway. What's the next town we'll be coming up to?"

I turned on the interior light of the car. "That would be...Hope," I said, tracing the snaky red line of the highway in the map book.

"Good a place to stay as any."

By the time we dragged ourselves into the Hope Hotel, all three of us were completely exhausted.

"We need a room, please," Dad said. "With three beds."

"All I have left is a single room and a double room," said the lady behind the counter. She had unnaturally bright red hair and cakey, overdone makeup.

Dad narrowed his eyes at Roy and me. Then he stared hard at Roy. Roy became really interested in picking a piece of lint off his shirt. "All right," Dad sighed. "I guess that will have to do." He paid for the rooms, then turned to us. "You kids hungry?"

"Yeah," we answered in unison.

"Do you have room service?" Dad asked Strawberry Shortcake.

"No," She snickered.

"Oh. Do you think maybe you could order us a pizza then?"

Her plastery face softened. "Sure, honey. I can do that. What do you want on it?"

After we'd eaten, Roy said goodnight to me and Dad. He hugged me extra tight and whispered in my ear, "I'll leave my door unlocked for you." Then he walked down the hall to his room. My heart fluttered inside my chest, and I had to cover my grin with my hand so Dad wouldn't see.

Dad lay on the bed, flicking through TV channels. "You go ahead and shower up first."

"Okay."

I showered and dressed for bed. When I came out of the bathroom, Dad was snoring loudly. I turned off the TV and the lights and crawled under the covers. I waited for about ten minutes to make sure he was asleep, then tiptoed out the door and went to Roy's room.

I knocked on the door.

"Come in." He cleared his throat.

I stepped inside. He was watching TV.

"Hey."

"Hey."

"What are you watching?"

"I think it's a fishing show." He laughed.

I laughed too

"Come on in. It's pretty funny, actually." He patted a spot on the bed beside him.

The room smelled faintly of urine, the ceiling had water stains, and the double bed had a horrible floral-print bedspread. The springs creaked as I sat down. Roy set up some pillows behind him and stretched out on the bed, and I did the same. The show was kind of funny, but I couldn't stop yawning.

"You tired?" Roy asked.

"Yeah. You?"

"I could sleep."

I smiled.

He switched off the TV and the bedside light. He was closing the blinds as I slipped under the covers. I lay in the dark with my eyes half open, listening to him undo his belt buckle and watching as he folded his clothes neatly and placed them on the chair. Then Roy slid under the sheets next to me. We both lay on our backs, watching shadows dance across the ceiling. The noise of traffic from the highway below almost sounded like waves rolling in.

I turned over onto my side, my back to Roy. He draped his arm across my belly and scooted closer so the front of his body pressed up against my back. He held me, and I let him.

In the morning he was still wrapped around me, and I felt a warm glow mushrooming inside my chest. I closed my eyes and wondered how much longer we could stay like this. Then Roy began to shift behind me and I sighed, because he was awake and the spell was broken.

He kissed me on the shoulder. "Good morning, sunshine."

"Morning," I groaned.

He pulled on my shoulder to roll me over, and then, propped on one arm, he leaned in and kissed me.

Even though we both had morning breath and sleep boogers in our eyes, we made out right there in the hotel bed. I didn't even have anything covering my head. It was bald as an egg, my head more naked than naked, and here I was being kissed and caressed by my boyfriend. It was fantastic.

We were interrupted way too soon by a rap on the door.

"Tamar! Are you in there? Time to get going, guys!" Dad sounded impatient but not furious, and for that I was grateful.

Roy kept kissing me, and I had to push him away to talk. "Okay! We'll be right there!"

Then Roy pounced on me and kissed me again like he was drowning and I was oxygen.

seventeen

We went to breakfast at a greasy spoon across the street. Dad looked at me with question marks in his eyes, but I avoided his gaze and stared out at the gently sloping mountains that were every shade of green.

In the car, we were already picking up Vancouver radio stations. The music was good, and the drive didn't seem so hard anymore. We bypassed Vancouver proper and went straight to the ferry terminal, where we boarded the tiny foot-passenger ferry to Stellar's Island at eleven o'clock. A tinny recorded announcement told us that our sailing time would be approximately seventy-five minutes and that, should we need them, there were life jackets under our seats. I pulled off my seat cover to check. There was nothing there but a dark empty space, some cobwebs and a gum wrapper. It was not reassuring.

Roy and I left Dad sprawled out across three seats with the newspaper and went outside to the upper deck. Staring out over the vastness of the Pacific, the faint purple shadows of distant mountains shimmering on the horizon, I wondered how it was possible that I had lived in Alberta all my life and never ventured into the neighboring province of British Columbia. It made me want to see all of BC, all of Canada, all of the world! Who knew there was so much beauty outside of Kananaskis Country and the badlands of Drumheller?

Roy and I walked around the upper deck, holding hands. Seagulls floated overhead on invisible air currents, suspended in time and space. The waves glittered ultramarine in the sun, and at that moment, I was happy. I really was.

After we docked, we got a cab to the hospital. The woman at reception told us Mom was in stable condition and could be discharged that day. Dad and I went to see her, leaving Roy in the waiting room flipping through *Popular Science*.

My mom was propped up in bed and watching a nature documentary about lions. "Tamar! David!" She opened her arms wide, scattering the crackers on her lap.

I ran to her and buried my face in her chest. A sudden, violent sobbing overtook me. I was not prepared for it, and I could not stop. It was like there was some agonized alien creature living inside me that had chosen this moment to burst forth onto the pale-blue hospital bedsheets.

My dad limped over and ran his hand over my back. "Shh, it's okay now, we're all okay now." He smoothed my mom's hair away from her face, and when I saw him look at her, I knew it was true.

I straightened up and composed myself. I remembered why we were here. My mom had a dark purple hoofprint in the center of her forehead. But she was alive, and she wasn't brain-dead or brainwashed or anything else we had been afraid to think about on the drive here. Her hair was longer than when I'd last seen her, and there were new silver strands around her face. There was a clarity in her eyes that I hadn't seen for a long time.

"Mom?"

"Yeah, honey?"

"I missed you."

She smiled, and the corners of her eyes crinkled up. Her eyes were shining with tears as she pulled me close to her again. "I missed you too, baby."

"Let's go home," Dad said.

Everyone was pretty quiet on the drive back to Calgary. Mom and Dad dozed in the backseat, and Roy and I listened to music and talk radio. Roy had to stop for a coffee every few hours. He insisted on getting us back to Calgary that night.

"I know I can get us there—it's only another five hours," he said, passing an RV.

"It doesn't matter, Roy. We can stop anytime. It's okay if we don't get back tonight," Dad said.

"I wish you could drive," Roy said to me.

"Me too," I sighed.

"Do you want to try?"

I looked at his face, lit up every few seconds by passing headlights. "Are you serious? We're on the number one! I've only ever scooted around in parking lots before. I can't do this. No. No way."

"No problem. Just checking, that's all."

I snorted.

"Maybe I could take you out a few times when we're back, get you comfortable on the road. You have your learner's license, don't you?"

"I was just about to take my test when my sisters..."

"Oh."

"So I never got it."

"That's...too bad."

"Yeah."

"Do you think your parents will ever let you drive?"

"It's highly doubtful."

"Damn."

"Double damn."

He laughed and so did I. He looked over at me. "You're even prettier when you laugh, you know that?"

"Eyes on the road, Roy!" Dad piped up from the back-seat, suddenly awake.

Both of us blushed, and I rolled my eyes. Roy squinted into the brights of an oncoming truck.

I stayed awake the whole trip to make sure Roy didn't fall asleep at the wheel. We finally got back to Calgary around four o'clock in the morning.

Dad thanked Roy profusely and slipped him a wad of bills. At first Roy tried to refuse, but Dad forced the cash into his hand. Then Mom and Dad helped each other into our house and left Roy and me standing in the driveway.

"Thank you so much, for everything," I said. "You're so..."

"What?"

"Great. You're so great. Thank you."

"Hey, no sweat. It was fun. We'll do it again sometime."

I laughed.

"Maybe just the two of us though."

"Okay."

"Go check out some Vancouver apartments."

"Yeah?"

"Why not?"

I couldn't stop smiling.

Then Roy reached for me and pulled me in close. We kissed, and it was warm and soft and delicious. The streetlights buzzed above us, and I felt something inside me melting.

"You should get some sleep," I said, pulling back.

"One more." He leaned in and kissed me again. Then he got into the little red car and I watched him drive away as the night tilted toward morning.

eighteen

We all slept until late in the afternoon. I didn't have to go to school. Then we had a big breakfast: banana pancakes, bacon, eggs, fruit. Mom ground up a bunch of spices and made us chai tea, something she had learned to make at The Yoga Farm. It was milky sweet but also spicy. Delicious. We watched a corny movie and ate popcorn and played Jenga. It was nice to have my family back together—what was left of it anyway.

On Saturday I worked at Mik's Milk and Gas. The sky was a great gray cotton ball, threatening to rain.

Between customers, Scott and I had contests to see who could make the best slushie combination. I got bonus points for most colorful: pink cream soda, orange crush, lemon ice and blueberry blast. But Scott's tasted better: Coke with cherry on top.

Around one thirty, Barney came in. Barney had to be pushing ninety. Wisps of white hair poked out of his mesh trucker's hat. He came in every Saturday at the same time to play "his numbers." He played Lotto 649 with the same six numbers every week, no extra. He had probably been playing those numbers every Saturday since the lottery was invented. I don't know if he's ever won. I doubt it, since he drives an ancient rust bucket and always wears the same clothes, a red plaid jacket and brown corduroy pants. I sighed as Barney left, ticket clutched tightly in his withered hand.

"What's wrong?" Scott asked.

"I don't know. Something about Barney depresses me."

"Why?"

"Because he's never going to win."

"Maybe he will, maybe he won't, but you know what he *has* got?"

"What?"

"Hope."

I nodded. Then two trucks and a car pulled in for gas, and Scott went out to fill them.

I barely heard the *beep-beep* of the door opening anymore, but I did notice it when a short guy dressed all in black and wearing pantyhose over his head came in. He reached behind him and locked the door. *Oh God oh God oh God what now?* I pressed the emergency button that hung around my neck and held it down. He pulled a gun out of his jacket and leveled it at my face. There was one other person in the store, a fat red-headed kid by the slushie machine, filling a giant cup.

"Open the cash drawer!" The man walked up to the counter and kept the gun pointed at my forehead. Then he turned it on the red-headed kid. "Don't try to be a hero, bucko!" He turned back to me. "Are you deaf? I said open the fucking drawer!" He slammed his fist against the counter.

"I—I can't open it."

"Don't fuck around with me, girl. I will kill you without batting an eyelash." He held the gun an inch away from my eye.

I stared into the black abyss of the barrel. I swallowed. My knees began to wobble so violently that I was afraid I was going to fall down. "It doesn't open it unless I make a sale or...or...or scan something through."

"Jesus." He picked up a pack of gum from the shelf and threw it on the counter. "Here."

I scanned it with shaking hands and pressed the cash button. The drawer popped open. The man kept the gun trained on my face. I looked past it and out the window. I could see that Scott's back was to me as he filled a big truck hauling a horse trailer. He looked to be having an animated conversation with the driver. Useless, totally useless.

"Come on! Move it! Move it! Move it!" The guy banged his hand against the counter again. "Take out the drawer! Dump the money in a bag! NOW!"

I bent to get a plastic bag. The phone rang. My heart seized. I looked at the phone. It was right beside my hand.

"Don't answer that!"

I looked at the phone again. It was so close. I could just press the Talk button and it would stop ringing, and whoever was calling would be able to hear what was happening and send help. It was right there. I didn't press it though. I stood up. The phone kept ringing. I looked at the red-headed kid. The shrill of the phone finally stopped as we stared at each other. The kid took a noisy sip of his slushie and swallowed, his eyes bulging out of his head. Then the phone started ringing again.

"LET'S GO!" the robber yelled, smacking the gun against the counter.

I dumped the contents of the cash drawer into the plastic bag, and he grabbed it out of my hand. He turned around, pulled off the pantyhose, unlocked the door and walked out. As if he were just another customer, carrying a bag full of junk food. The phone was silent. Everything was silent.

I sat down with a thud behind the counter. Everything spun around me. I stared at the phone. Then I picked it up and dialled 9-1-1.

"Nine-one-one, what is your emergency?"

"I've just been robbed."

"Are you injured?"

I looked down at my body. My hands were shaking, my knees were shaking, and I wanted to vomit. "No," I said. "I...I'm okay."

"Is anyone else injured?"

I peered over the counter at the red-headed kid. He was staring out the window after the robber and gulping down his slushie like he was dying of thirst. "No," I said.

"Just sit tight, ma'am. The police are on their way."

After I'd hung up, I took off my emergency-button necklace, threw it on the floor and stomped on it until it was broken in a million little pieces. Then I took off my Mik's hat, tossed it on the counter, grabbed my purse and walked out the door.

"Hey, Tamar! Where are you going?" Scott yelled after me.

"I QUIT!"

As I walked home, I watched the sunset unfurl like a dying rose. My heart was like a jackhammer inside my chest. Everything looked blurred around the edges. I felt cold and sick to my stomach. *Just keep walking. Go home. Go home.* I tried to focus on my breath. In. Out. In…and out. I couldn't get it back to normal. But I was breathing, I was still alive.

When I opened the door, my mom and dad were sitting on the couch playing cards. One look at my mom, and I crumbled.

"Tamar, what's the matter?"

I fell into my mom's lap and exploded into tears.

"Shh, it's okay, honey. I'm here now. Don't cry." She smoothed my bare scalp with her hand.

"What is it? What's wrong?" Dad asked.

"Tell us what happened, Tamar. Did somebody hurt you?"

I nodded yes, but I couldn't stop crying. I couldn't believe what had just happened to me, but I was bawling too hard to tell them. Tears and snot sprayed out of me in all directions. It took me about half an hour to calm down. When I finally got it out, they were horrified.

"I'm calling the police!" Dad said.

"I already did," I said.

"I'm calling them again then."

"Why? What's the point?"

"I'm calling the store!" Mom said.

"No. It's done. It's over now."

They looked at each other and moved to be on either side of me. Then they wrapped themselves around me like a blanket. I closed my eyes and let myself be held. Together, we waited for the tremors to subside.

nineteen

After I had calmed down enough, Mom made me change into my pajamas, even though it was only five thirty. She made me chamomile tea and toast with butter and honey. Eventually, I stopped shaking.

Scott called later that night to see if I was okay. He had figured out what had happened, and I guess the red-headed kid had stuck around long enough to puke up his slushie and talk to the cops. Scott had called the owner, Pete, and Pete didn't even let him close down the store. He brought in a new float and put the pumps on self-serve so Scott could keep working by himself.

"Tamar, I am so sorry."

"It's not your fault."

"I should have been in there with you. I could have done something."

"There was nothing you could have done, Scott. I'm just glad I wasn't shot to death."

"Oh god, me too! I never would have been able to forgive myself. I am *so* sorry this happened to you. I never would have...I never thought—"

"I'll survive. I always do."

"Let me know if there's anything I can do. If you need anything, anything at all."

"Okay."

"Just call me. Anytime, day or night."

"All right. Thanks."

"Promise me you'll call me if you need anything, even just someone to talk to."

"I promise."

"Oh, and Tamar?"

"What?"

"The police said they need to talk to you too. To help them fill out their incident report or whatever. I said I'd tell you to call them."

"Okay."

Yes, I was shattered. Traumatized, even. But, on the upside, the whole experience had made me feel lucky to be alive, and I hadn't felt that way in a long, long time.

I was glad it was the weekend, because I just wanted to chill. It actually turned out to be a long weekend for me, because the parents and I decided I shouldn't go to school on Monday. It was nice having Mom back home, and Dad was coming around to his old self again, finally. He'd had his cast taken off and we all went for a little walk through the flat part of Fish Creek Park together. The trees were popping out their bright green buds and the creek was higher than I had ever seen it. We saw a buck and doe with their awkward new fawn, ten or fifteen black squirrels and a bunch of different birds, including a red-winged blackbird.

When we got home, Mom and I made a big pot of chili and Dad made bread. After dinner, we played Scrabble. I won with a triple-word score on the word *xenophobia*. Mom told us she had seen God during a meditation at the Yoga Farm, that they had made their peace and now she wasn't afraid anymore.

"What did God look like?" I asked.

"Like the brightest star you've ever seen."

"Like the sun?"

"Brighter."

On Tuesday morning, I was dressed and down in the kitchen eating cereal at seven thirty. But I had accidentally poured orange juice on my cereal and milk in my glass. I was still getting used to the whole breakfast thing. I decided to eat it anyway, as it all goes down the same hole. My mom sat down at the table across from me with her coffee and looked at my bowl.

"Are you going to be okay?" she asked.

"Yeah, probably."

"You don't have to go to school today if you don't want to. We can just take it easy for a while."

"I should probably just go. I can't hide away from the world forever."

She smiled. "I'm proud of you, Tamar."

I pushed my orange-y flakes around in my bowl.

Later, as I was going out the door, my mom said, "Hey, Tamar, it's a little chilly out today. Maybe you want to wear a toque?" She handed me a black cap. I pulled it on and realized I had almost left for school with a naked head. Maybe tomorrow I would. After staring down the barrel of a loaded gun, somehow being bald didn't seem like such a big deal anymore.

Roy came up to my locker at first bell.

"Guess what I got this weekend?" he asked, grinning.

"Uh, robbed at gunpoint?"

"No…"

"Oh, because that would have been a coincidence."

"What?"

"Because I did."

"*What?*"

I nodded and bit my lower lip.

"Are you serious?"

"Serious as a heart attack."

"Holy shit! Tamar! Are you okay?"

"I think so. I didn't get shot anyway."

"Oh my god. I can't believe this. Why didn't you call me?"

I shrugged. "What could you have done?"

"I could have been there for you."

"My family was there."

"But—"

"It's okay, Roy."

"Jesus." He put his arms around me and held me tight. I could feel him shaking his head in disbelief.

After a minute or two, I pulled away. "So what's your news?"

"Oh, it's nothing."

"No, come on, tell me."

"I got two tickets to the Pink Floyd Laser Light Show in July, that's all."

"What? *Really?* That's awesome!"

He nodded, a micro grin curling up the corners of his lips.

"How did you get those?"

"Do you know anyone who would want to go with me?" He looked up and down the hallway, pretending to search for someone to take.

"Yeah." I hit him lightly in the chest. "Me!" I couldn't help bouncing up and down. I couldn't help giving him a giant smack of a kiss on the lips.

twenty

It seemed like July would never come. I was still thinking of moving to Vancouver with Roy at the end of the summer, but I didn't mention anything to the parents about it. They were busy. They were repainting the kitchen. A warm, sunny yellow, Mom called it. Actually, it was more like the color of urine, but no one asked my opinion. They both spoke of going back to work soon. They had begun to sort through Abby's and Alia's things, deciding what to keep, what to donate and what to throw away. They talked about making some sort of presentation at high schools about drinking and driving. They seemed sort of shy around each other, tentative. As if they were just getting to know one another instead of having been married for twenty years already.

Dad said if anything happened to me before the concert, he would have to go in my place. I think he was a little jealous that I was going, but he had gotten to see Pink Floyd on their Wish You Were Here tour in 1975.

The first Friday in May, we had the dress rehearsal of *The Wizard of Oz* and performed it for the Canyon Meadows Elementary kids. I wore my Auntie Em wig, which was gray and curly, and actually didn't look too bad. I wasn't that nervous—the audience was only about twenty twerpy little kids, after all.

There were a few screwups but nothing major. The lighting was sketchy in some places. The spotlight didn't come on over the right part of the stage and had to sweep across it twice to find the person it was aiming for. Our techie wasn't the sharpest tool in the shed, as they say.

In our notes afterward, Ms. Jane told me to smile more.

On Saturday night, I *was* nervous. I left almost all of the food on my plate at dinner.

"Why aren't you eating? You need to eat," Dad said.

"I can't. I might throw up."

"Why would you throw up?" Mom asked.

"Opening-night jitters." I shrugged.

"T, don't be ridiculous. You know all your lines. You did fine in your rehearsal, right? What do you have to be nervous about?"

"I don't know? The fact that I'll be on display for everyone to stare at. If I screw up, I could ruin the entire play. Anything could happen, and everyone would see. I could trip, fall on my face, a spotlight could fall on my head—"

"Tamar, honey, relax. Okay? Deep breaths. Here, try this. Cover your right nostril with your thumb and inhale through your left nostril."

I did as she showed me.

"Good. Now cover the left nostril and exhale through the right. Good, good, that's it. Now, inhale right and exhale left."

"What are you doing?" Dad laughed.

"It's called *nadi shodhana*, alternate-nostril breathing. It's a calming yogic technique," Mom said sharply.

He put up his hands. "Just asking, that's all."

"I think it's working," I said.

"Of course it is," Dad said, rolling his eyes. "When you're finished that, I want you to eat at least six more bites of your dinner, or else you'll have no energy left for Auntie Em."

"Okay, okay."

"And I want to help you with your makeup," Mom said.

"We have people for that, Mom. They have to use the really thick theater stuff. It's not normal makeup."

"Well, I'll do your eyebrows then."

"Okay, whatever."

"And don't forget to call your grandma so she can tell you to break a leg," Dad said.

"Do I have to? I have to go pretty soon; you know how she goes on."

"Yes, you have to."

"And don't forget to pee before you go onstage," Mom said. "That will help with the jitters."

"OKAY!"

Twenty minutes later, I slammed out the door to go get my makeup and hair done and get into costume. On the walk to school, I thought about how, even though they could be irritating as hell, they were cute, my parents, in their own way.

Roy was my best friend, my boyfriend, my Rock of Gibraltar, and I had no idea how I was going to get through my last year of high school without him, but how could I leave my parents right now? They were so fragile.

My costume looked good, my wig looked good, and Marika, the makeup artist, assured me that my makeup would look great from far away. I had on dark-mauve lipstick to make my mouth stand out, fat gray eyebrows, thick black eyeliner and tons of mascara, and heavy, heavy taupe foundation. As I was getting the rosiest pink cheeks in the world painted on, there was a loud knock on the door of the dressing room.

"Yeah?" Marika yelled as she dusted my face with powder.

A bald man stepped into the room. "Special delivery!" he said. He held a bouquet of flowers in one hand, and in the other, a single red rose.

"Thanks," Marika said. "Just set them on the table there." She continued powdering me.

The other girls in the room stared at the flowers. Every female in the cast was in there, and two other makeup artists. Marika glanced at the cards on the flowers. "They're for you," she said.

I stared into the mirror, and everyone else stared at me.

When my hair and makeup were finished, I smelled the rose and then read the cards. The rose was from Roy, and the card said *You are a star, don't ever forget it.* I twirled the rose around in my fingers and inhaled its scent. The bouquet was from the parents, and the card read *Break a leg tonight, T. Break both legs! We're so proud of you!*

Even though every girl in the room was glaring at me like she wanted to scratch out my eyeballs, I couldn't help grinning like a proper fool.

"Places! Places, everyone!" Ms. Jane used her stage whisper.

I couldn't see a damn thing, only the green glow tape marking the stage exits, but I could hear the excited buzz of the audience, the hammering of my heart and a dull hum inside my head. Ms. Jane went out front and made an enthusiastic welcome speech. There was wild applause and then absolute silence. The curtain went up. I squinted past the blinding lights into the audience. Every seat in the house was full. And there, front row and center, sat the three people I loved. I knew, too, that when the curtain came down, my sisters, wherever they were, would be giving me a standing ovation.

acknowledgments

THANK YOU:
Staff and students of Dr. E.P. Scarlett High School, 1999-2001, especially Margie Johnson and Jane Pilkey; Lynn Coady for suggesting my short story "Dr. Lung" should grow into this novel; John Gould and Nancy Holmes; Kelda Larson and David Floody for reading an early draft; Sarah Harvey for fine editing; my family for their unflagging enthusiasm and support; Mom and Dad, the best parents a kid could ask for; and Warren, who makes everything possible.

Ashley Little attended high school in Calgary. She has worked at a pie shop, a fast-food chicken restaurant and a convenience store/gas station. She completed a BFA in creative writing at the University of Victoria. Ashley teaches yoga and writes fiction in Alberta's badlands. For more information, please visit www.ashleylittle.com.